The Gilded Coach

The Gilded Coach

by

Isabell Rae Habersham

First Fiction Series

SUNSTONE
PRESS

SANTA FE

Sunstone books may be purchased for educational, business, or sales promotional use. For information please write: Special Markets Department, Sunstone Press, P.O. Box 2321, Santa Fe, New Mexico 87504-2321.

Library of Congress Cataloging-in-Publication Data:

Habersham, Isabella Rae, 1916–
    The gilded coach / by Isabella Rae Habersham.
      p. cm. –(First fiction series)
ISBN: 0-86534-348-9
      1. South Carolina—History—Colonial period, ca. 1600–1775—Fiction.
2. Anglo-Spanish War, 1739–1748—Fiction. I. Title. II. Series.

PS3608.A24 G45 2002
813'.54—dc21   2002018800

Published in   SUNSTONE PRESS
Post Office Box 2321
Santa Fe, NM 87504-2321 / USA
(505) 988-4418 / *orders only* (800) 243-5644
FAX (505) 988-1025
www.sunstonepress.com

Contents

1

Passage to America

"Do you, Margaret Staud, confess to the heinous sin of bigamy?"

Margaret heard the sonorous voice of Pastor Boltzius, which was followed by a faint and distant, "I do."

"And do you know that, if you do not truly repent, you will lose both body and soul?"

Lose both body and soul! Margaret, or Margo as she was affectionately called, had heard these very words somewhere before. Yes, it was at Neus on the Rhine back in 1738, when her Swiss traveling party met the funny little English clergyman who tried to discourage them from going to Carolina.

"And now that you have confessed and repented for this vile sin," the stern-faced minister continued, "God, through Christ's merits, will forgive you this transgression if only you recognize your depravity and crawl like a little worm into the merciful wounds of Jesus. Do you truly repent?"

"I truly repent," Margo answered in a somewhat stronger voice.

"Then you are hereby forgiven, and your sin is relegated to oblivion. Should anyone mention it, the guilt will fall upon him." Her church penance finally completed, Margo returned to her reveries and ignored the sermon Pastor Boltzius had now begun and would surely continue for another hour. Johann Martin Boltzius was the clergyman assigned to a congregation of Salzburgers who had been expelled by their archbishop because they would not renounce their Protestant faith. They had settled at Ebenezer, some twenty-five miles upstream from the year-old town of Savannah.

∼

While the prolix pastor droned on about adultery and fornication, Margo recalled that beautiful day at Neus on the Rhine. She, her father

Franz Stehli, her mother Trudi, and her two little brothers, Marti and Sali, were in high spirits, even though they had run out of money.

"Why are we out of money, Daddy?" little Marti asked, looking up adoringly at his father.

"Because everything costs more than we expected."

The journey to the Rhine and down that river to Neus had been far more expensive than the newlander, Hans Jacob Riemensperger, had anticipated or admitted. When recruiting emigrants at twelve shillings a head for the voyage to South Carolina, Riemensperger had not warned them of the many tolls demanded along the Rhine, where travelers had to pay a tax on themselves and everything they had with them. The worst of these was the "Mousetower on the Rhine," the little toll tower standing on an island in the middle of the river.

"Did the mice really eat up Bishop Hatto?" Marti asked.

"No," Franz answered, "his own people chased him to the tower and killed him because he had been so greedy. People blamed the mice because they thought the name Mauteturm meant 'mouse tower' instead of 'toll tower'. Riemensperger says there are no tolls in Carolina. You can go up and down the Ashley or the Savannah Rivers as much as you want and never have to pay a toll."

This was one of the few truthful things the dealer in human cargoes ever said.

By now the Stehlis had little to declare, having exchanged most of their belongings for food along the way. The two boys had been barefoot for more than a month and Margo's shoes were falling to pieces.

Because of his financial anxieties, Franz looked much older than his forty years. He slouched forward when walking, perhaps as a result of having plowed too young, before his bones had properly developed. He was wearing a full beard, dark brown with some streaks of gray.

Franz's beard made people along the way think he was some sort of religious enthusiast because beards were out of fashion. They were worn mostly by dissenters like the Amish and Mennonites, many of whom were then going down the Rhine on their way to the island of Pennsylvania in the West Indies. Franz was no dissenter. He was unshaven because he

8

had sold his ancestral razor when paying off his debts.

Trudi also looked older than her years because of the drudgery of maintaining a hard-scrabble farm. Although Margo had worked hard, too, her youth made her energetic and vivacious. While walking she circled her parents like a well-trained bird dog.

~

Franz had not wished to sell his farm, a little parcel of land only a few miles from Lützelflüh in Switzerland's Canton Bern; but he had incurred crushing debts despite all his back-breaking work and frugality. His neighbor uphill from him, pressed by his creditors, had risked plowing up his meadow land to plant a cash crop.

"Don't you think your soil's too shallow to plow?" Franz had asked him.

"I'm afraid you may be right," the neighbor conceded, adding sadly, "I've tried to convince my creditors but they are making me plant a money crop."

An unusual cloudburst washed away all the neighbor's plowed and harrowed top soil. The next downpour rushed across his naked fields and carried away the shallow soil of Franz's freshly planted wheat field. This made it impossible for him to borrow any more seed money from his factor in Lützelflüh. The neighbor concluded, "In the old days it was the nobility and clerics who robbed us farmers. Now it's the money-lenders in the cities who are crushing us."

When Franz at last auctioned his farm with its eroded field, it brought just enough to cover his debts and the estimated travel expenses to Carolina.

"We are not the only people in our parish to leave home," Franz said defensively to his family and friends. "At least six other families have been persuaded by Riemensperger, who has brought signed letters from Carolina attesting it's a veritable paradise where a second crop of wheat sprouts as soon as the first has been harvested."

"Does anyone know any of the people who wrote the letters?" a skeptical neighbor asked.

"I don't know, but we have no other choice."

After selling all their belongings they could not carry on their backs, the Stehlis joined Riemensperger's large group leaving for Carolina. Despite their sorrow at leaving the alpine farm where generations of Stehlis had lived, Franz and his family finally blended in with the carefree and optimistic traveling party, which contained many vagrants and field hands, as well as several respectable but impoverished peasant families such as themselves. All Switzerland was in the throes of the *rabies Carolinae* or Carolina madness, and the governments and landowners were doing all they could to stop the exodus of working people. Their emigration might encourage the remaining workers to demand a decent living wage.

"Why do you always drop out of line every time you see a fine carriage?" Trudi asked her daughter.

"I don't know, I guess I just like to see'em."

Margo had never told her family about her fantasy of someday owning an opulent carriage drawn by four splendid horses. The fantasy had begun years earlier, while she was minding her goats on an alpine meadow. A dazzlingly gilded carriage arrived, driven by a coachman accompanied by a postilion, both in livery. The two lackeys spread a cloth on the ground and covered it with bottles and baskets and then opened the carriage door and helped the gorgeously dressed passengers descend to eat their picnic lunch.

Margo had never seen such silk and satin finery. "I'm going to live like that some day," she swore audibly to herself. "Perhaps our move to Carolina will make it all come true."

By the time the Stehlis reached Neus they were in rags, living largely on public charity and from trivial sums borrowed at usurious rates from their conductor, Riemensperger. Yet the Stehlis' spirits were buoyed by their expectations of the wealth and comforts they would enjoy in Carolina.

"We will all work off our passage money and then buy a farm," Franz promised, "one much, much bigger than our old one." The Stehlis were a close-knit family, with no jealousies or sibling rivalries; and they thanked the Lord they would all be together in their new home.

John Wesley, the British clergyman they met in Neus, had just returned from South Carolina and Georgia. He tried eloquently to disabuse the emigrants of their fantasies.

"No, the streets of Carolina are not paved with gold," he insisted, "crops do not bear a hundredfold without cultivation. The weather, while seldom too cold, is usually so hot and unhealthy in summer that most Europeans there die promptly. Nor do their souls fare any better than their bodies in that godless land where there are no churches. If you persist in going there, you will lose *both body and soul*."

~

Upon arriving at Rotterdam, Franz indentured himself and his family to Capt. John Wadham of the *Europa*, who paid off Franz's debts to Riemensperger and added a year to the four years of servitude normally demanded for passage to America. Wadham did not look like a sea captain. He looked more like a country parson who drank too much port. His beetling black eyebrows should have been frightening, but weren't.

Wadham, who knew there was a ready market for redemptioners in Georgia, persuaded Stehli to settle in that new colony, South Carolina's southern neighbor.

"Fifty acres of land," he said, "are given free to every servant upon the completion of his service, and there are no slaves to compete against, as there are in Carolina."

The 190 ton *Europa* teemed with emigrants, mostly Swiss on their way to South Carolina, and Margo estimated there must be one passenger for every ton of ship. The little vessel was dreadfully overcrowded. It carried mostly South Germans and Swiss, with a few dissenters who spoke a strange North German dialect. The Stehlis were lucky. They had a whole bunk to themselves, a wooden shelf about six feet square, on which they could all sleep at the same time by lying spoon fashion.

Scarcely out of sight of Rotterdam, Franz noticed that his wife looked pale.

"What's the matter Trudi?"

His question was answered as soon as she ran to the rail. In a short time most of the passengers became seasick on the rough English Channel. All decks and ladders were awash in vomit, with hardly enough pails, mops, and able-bodied people to remove it.

Fortunately for the Stehlis, they had met Johann Staud, a farmer from Saarbruecken, who joined the traveling party at Neus and became Franz's bosom friend. Traveling alone, Johann helped Franz care for his ailing family. Staud was a large florid man. He looked fat, but the adipose was just a thin veneer over his hard muscles. He was very self-possessed and spoke little.

By the time the *Europa* reached Dover the seasickness was at last over. Margo was disappointed that the passengers could not leave the crowded ship and stroll in the town, but Captain Wadham was afraid his German redemptioners might take French leave. Besides, he wished them to clean up the remaining vomit. The delay in port was uncomfortable, even if rather short.

Several weeks out of Dover a variant of typhus broke out, a disease commonly called Palatine fever.

"Why's it called Palatine fever?" Marti asked his father, who was holding him on his lap.

"Because it so often strikes the Palatines on their way to America," the father answered, fondly patting his son's head.

"And who are the Palatines?" the child asked.

"They're the people who live around Heidelberg and Kaiserslautern, but the English use the word to mean any German workers, no matter where they come from. Even we Swiss are sometimes called Palatines."

～

Most of the passengers not down with typhus were afflicted by the bloody flux, as dysentery was then called; and the entire ship reeked of blood and human feces. In time, the stench of death surpassed even that of blood and feces. Franz was the first of his family to succumb to the plague. Staud bartered some trade goods with a sailor in exchange for enough stolen sail cloth to wrap up the body, which was quietly dropped overboard with a benediction by Captain Wadham.

Unto Almighty God we commend the soul of our brother
departed, and we commit his body to the deep; in sure
and certain hope of the Resurrection unto eternal life . . .

12

The Swiss could not understand the words, but the captain's rich and solemn voice impressed them deeply. His epaulets, wig, decorations, and three-cornered hat were also imposing. This was the first time he had worn them on the voyage.

Trudi was the next in the family to go, but Staud could get no shroud for her. Captain Wadham could not read the funeral service because he was sick in his bunk below, so a common seaman did the best he could with the King's English.

Staud could get no shroud of any kind for the two boys, who followed their mother into the sea a few days later. Sali died in Margo's tight embrace.

"You must let go of Sali now," Staud pleaded. "He's tired and wants to go to sleep."

Margo looked at Staud with blank and feverish eyes and clung to her little brother even more tightly. Staud had to break her grip to take the little corpse away from her and to the gunnel, where a Swiss layman said a prayer as they dropped the emaciated body overboard. Margo was still unconscious when Marti, the older brother, died a day later.

Only Margo survived the disease, which was complicated by the scurvy resulting from lack of fresh food. Staud moved to her bunk to be on hand for every need.

"Here's some hot broth for you, Margo," Staud coaxed, holding a spoon to her lips. With much luck he had caught some of the flying fish that fell on the deck, and he had bribed the cook to make the broth. Later he bought a bit of shark liver from the sailors. On another occasion he bought some flesh of a porpoise the sailors had harpooned.

While Death still ruled the ill-fated ship, a violent storm almost demolished it. Waves as high as houses dropped the little craft into a deep trough and then hurled it upward to the crest of the next great foamy wave, only to smash into the sea again and again. Stout tied Margo to her bunk and then went to help the crew, many of them dangerously sick. Only the small party of North Germans remained composed and sang songs of praise to the Lord, while most of the other passengers were screaming with despair.

13

As soon as the storm subsided and the weather turned fair, Captain Wadham, now almost recovered, appeared on deck and commanded: "Reef sails and launch all dinghies." His voice was as deep as his chest.

"Aye, aye, Sir," all hands answered.

"Anyone strong enough can go swimming. We are in the Gulf Stream and the water is warm."

Many men swam in their clothes, sometimes after soaking them in the urine barrel to cut the grime. Because of so many deaths and because the journey was nearing its end, Wadham could be a bit more generous with water and rations. As a result, the urine barrel remained full. The men relieved themselves directly into the barrel, which was lashed to the bowsprit, while the women passed up chamber pots from below decks.

"Those passengers and crewmen who are strong enough to do so will haul up buckets of sea water for swabbing the ladders, cabins, and lower decks." The broad-shouldered Captain Wadham had recovered his stentorian command voice and needed no bullhorn. "Those finding no buckets will take turns on the pumps to get rid of the stinking bilge. By sunset the ship will no longer smell like a slaver."

～

When the *Europa* finally reached Savannah, Staud smuggled his skin-and-bones patient past the quarantine guard.

"Where ya taking that person to?" the suspicious old sentry demanded, taking a closer look.

"I'm going to bury her," Staud answered in his memorized English. "She's dead, can't you see? I'm fixin' to bury her." He carried Margo to the hut of two German Swiss women he had met in town that morning.

Augusta Schneider and her daughter Liesbeth, both widows, received the sick girl into their home and nursed her back to health. In reporting the *Europa*'s tragic voyage to the Georgia Trustees, Col. William Stephens, their new secretary in Georgia, praised the "courageous Dutch wives" for their kindness to the poor sick Swiss. The Trustees were the philanthropic gentlemen in London who were sponsoring the colony of Georgia.

The Schneider women looked like sisters, both slender and vigor-

14

ous. The younger one had lost her husband on the passage over three years earlier and the older one had lost hers soon after reaching Savannah. The daughter was called Liesbeth, but her mother was always called the Widow Schneider, or Snyder by the English. They were accomplished seamstresses and laundresses and served all the British officials.

Margo's rapid recovery resulted in part from the fresh vegetables and fruit brought her by Staud, whose ruddy coloring betrayed no trace of the disastrous epidemics on the voyage.

"Where did you get all this?" Margo asked him.

"From a fellow shipmate now working at the Trustees' Garden. That's where they test crops and fruits for the new colony."

~

When all the sick had been provided for, Johann Staud, or John Stout as he was now called, was allocated as a servant to John Milledge, who had arrived as a lad of ten on the *Anne,* the first ship to Savannah. In some five years he had become a hardy and handsome young man.

"During the last four years," the raw-boned Augusta Schneider told Stout, "Milledge has lost both parents and has thus become the head of his household, consisting of a younger brother and a still younger sister."

In time the servant Stout, aged thirty-eight, became a father-figure for his master, John Milledge, aged sixteen, whom he served faithfully. Their relationship was like that of an old and respectful petty officer and his inexperienced ensign. While rigidly respectful, the subordinate could be very severe when advising his superior.

Margo gradually recovered her glowing health and striking beauty. Her dark-lashed blue eyes sparkled once more, and her rich raven hair again contrasted pleasingly with the pink whiteness of her face and neck. Like all the other passengers, she had suffered from scurvy.

"How did you keep your teeth?" the older widow Schneider asked.

"I tried not to use them. I soaked my bread in the little water they gave us, and I cut up the chunks of meat so small that I could swallow them unchewed." As a result of her care, all her pearly teeth were still intact and her gums were once again rosy red. Above all, she had regained her lost weight.

"You've sure done a good job fattening her up," Stout complimented the Schneiders. "She doesn't look like the skinny corpse I brought ashore. Looks like a grown woman." Still slender, Margo was curvaceous and her breasts were unusually well developed for her age. Despite her gain in weight, she still had a wasp waist.

As soon as Margo was strong enough to work, Colonel Stephens assigned her as maid servant and field hand to the Schneider women for four and a half years. They buried her undergarments and boiled the rest of her clothes for two hours in rainwater with wood ash, thus salvaging her green dirndl skirt and red bodice, both a bit paler and tighter than before the boiling. All her and her family's meager clothing and other belongings had been confiscated by the ship's bursar to pay toward their unpaid passage. That was in the contract, which Franz had not been able to read.

~

One pleasantly warm evening Stout asked Margo, "What were you thinking of while you were delirious? You kept repeating some word that sounded like gilded coach." Margo told him about the ornate coach, which had now become a symbol of all her worldly ambitions.

"Well, you won't find any fine coaches in Savannah," the clean-shaven shipmate assured her, "a few carts, perhaps, but no coaches or carriages."

"Why not?"

"No roads for them. There's a cart trail from Savannah to Oxstead, Causton's plantation, and one from Savannah to Whitefield's orphanage at Bethesda and from there to Bewlie, Colonel Stephen's plantation. I guess that shows who's important around here.

"Building the orphanage is the biggest business in town," Stout added, "he pays eighteen pence per day for labor, and no one else can compete. Even some of the Salzburgers come down to work for him."

Savannah had not grown much since its initial founding some five years earlier. The houses, all uniform, were of sawed timber, fourteen by twenty-six feet, and covered with unplaned feather-edged boards. The roofs were of shingles and the floors of heavy puncheons, split logs with the flat surface turned up. The checkerboard plan of the city, which had been devised in London, allowed for future growth.

"What I like most about the town," Margo said, "are the squares along the main streets."

"These squares," Stout told her, "are called Trust Lots. They are to serve as village commons, where the people can tether their cattle until they make fences. They will also serve as camping grounds for refugees from the countryside in case of hostile attack. Eventually they'll be public parks."

Margo listened attentively to everything Stout said. She also saw the crane on the high bluff, which was so steep that freight had to be hauled up to the bluff by a crane and winch.

"It was while working on this crane," Stout informed Margo, "that Augusta Schneider's husband was killed. A poorly secured chest fell down on him. The workers at the crane are all Palatines indentured to the Trust and therefore called Trust Servants.

"Right over there," Stout continued, "was Oglethorpe's tent. He kept on living in his tent long after all of his subordinates were housed." No one in the colony could accuse James Edward Oglethorpe, the 'founder of Georgia', of not sharing their hardships.

Stout then led Margo to the Trustees' Garden, from which his friend had filched the fruit and vegetables that helped her back to health. The garden lay at the northeast corner of the town. Still sensitive about losing his farm near Saarbruecken, he hoped to prove to himself and to the world that the failure was not his fault. He would establish a far better farm in Georgia, and for this purpose he learned all he could from the Trustees' gardener.

"Ten acres," Stout said to his attentive friend. "Notice that there are all kinds of soil. For example, up here it's sandy like the rest of the town, but on the eastern slope it's a kind of clay, and along the marsh it is rich silt." Margo listened to all this carefully, for she was already hoping for a garden of her own. "The Trustees are not only introducing all kinds of tropical plants for the colonists," Stout added, "but also raising medical herbs for England."

The gardener came up and gave Margo some pears, for which he received an appreciative curtsy. As soon as the gardener left, Stout asked, "Did you hear about his wife?"

"No, what about her?"

"He married an Indian girl, very formally before the whole tribe and with an exchange of gifts, but two weeks later she tired of Savannah and went home again. No one has heard anything of her since."

A short distance west of the crane was Yamacraw Village, where a small group of Indians lived. A very minor tribe, just a fragment of the Creek Nation and not fully accepted by their more numerous kinsmen.

"Who's their head man?" Margo asked.

"Their old chief, Tomochichi," Stout replied. "He's a big man now among the Creeks because he befriended the English, from whom he can get guns, rum, and protection. The English even invited him and his entourage to meet the King in London, where Tomochichi was duly impressed by English power."

The Yamacraws were the first Indians Margo ever saw. Her visits to Yamacraw ceased abruptly after an ugly spectacle. An Indian brave cut off a widow's hair and ears and showed them around because she had been too familiar with an Englishman.

Margo had not yet seen an African. Slavery was forbidden in Georgia, along with rum and lawyers.

"Slaves sawed boards for the Salzburgers while they were building their settlement at Ebenezer," Augusta Schneider told her, "but they were all recalled to South Carolina as soon as they finished their task, all but one who had been knifed by a fellow slave."

"Why did he do that?"

"No idea," the Swiss woman answered. "They are often violent, especially towards each other."

"Do the people here want slavery?"

"Most of them don't, but there's an active group, mostly Lowland Scots, who want slavery. The Salzburgers and the Highlanders down the coast at Darien have both submitted petitions to the Trustees asking them not to permit slavery, since it would destroy their way of life." I would surely have signed the petition, too, Margo thought, if I had been here.

~

On two occasions each year Savannah burst into drunken merriment. One was Guy Fawkes Day, when the mob hanged an effigy of Fawkes from an improvised lamp post and 'there let him die'.

"Who was Guy Fawkes?" Margo asked.

"A fellow who tried to blow up the Parliament," a drunk and swaying bystander explained. "That's why we sing, 'Guy Fawkes, Guy, hang him on high. Hang him to a lamp post and there let him die'. Fawkes had a dozen barrels of powder under the building when they caught him."

The other merry celebration was the King's Birthday with numerous toasts drunk with spirits donated by the government. Many cannons were fired at this joyful festivity. Margo did not yet feel like participating, but she did enjoy seeing other people have fun.

During these frolics Margo made an interesting observation, which she shared with Mrs. Schneider. "All the German children who have lived in Savannah for several years speak English not only with the English children but also with each other. They also speak English to their parents, who understand English but answer in German. Their family conversations are often bilingual."

"In Ebenezer," Mrs. Schneider said, "the children speak only German because there are no English speakers to learn from."

~

John Milledge found a good use for John Stout, his new servant. George Whitefield, the famous evangelist, had just returned to Savannah from a tour throughout England and the northern colonies collecting funds for his orphanage at Bethesda, which lay some ten miles south of Savannah. He also brought gifts, including a church bell, for the Salzburgers. In Philadelphia it was said that even the pinch-penny Benjamin Franklin was unable to resist the persuasive preacher and emptied his pocket into the collection plate.

"By the grace of God the orphanage is at last completed," Whitefield announced with solemn self-satisfaction. What he didn't expect was the difficulty he would have finding enough orphans to fill it. All orphans in

19

Georgia and South Carolina were immediately claimed by their kinsmen, sometimes by distant kinsmen, because even very small children were useful on a farm. This was proved by Milledge's young siblings, Richard and Frances, who worked like Trojans.

When Whitefield learned that the Milledge children were being raised by their sixteen-year-old brother, he went straight to Colonel Stephens.

"A minor like that cannot possibly provide adequate Christian nurture to two small children. He is letting them grow up to be perfect heathens."

"Not exactly heathens," the stately colonel disagreed in his dignified manner. "He sends them to Sunday school regularly, whenever it's operating."

"But there's no mother at home to teach them their prayers," the religious enthusiast insisted.

Although not entirely convinced, Stephens allowed the zealous clergyman to take the two children to his orphanage. Stephens was still only Secretary to the Trustees, yet he was virtually the chief magistrate of Savannah and could act arbitrarily in the Trustees' name. During Margo's first year in Savannah the dedicated empire builder was promoted to President of the Council, thus making his authority official.

"I'm very unhappy about the strict discipline enforced at Whitefield's orphanage," young Milledge protested to Stephens. "Their long day is allotted strictly to work and prayer with never a moment for play or rest. Besides that, one of the pupils there was severely flogged by Chaplain Barber for writing a letter reporting bad treatment."

Offended that his position as head of household was being questioned, Milledge conspired with his servant Stout to rescue the children. Aided by the surveyor Noble Jones, who had meanwhile become the scoutboat skipper, Milledge landed one morning at Bethesda, well before dawn and even before morning prayers began, and spirited the children away from their dormitory and into the scout boat.

By the time Whitefield discovered their absence and reported it to Stephens, the children were safely hidden among some of the families of the "courageous Dutch wives", whom Stephens had so warmly praised. Margo, in the conspiracy for Stout's sake, had recruited a foster mother. Jones implied that the abduction was secretly encouraged by General Oglethorpe, who was then at his new fortress city Frederica on Saint Simons Island, which guarded the southern frontier of Georgia.

Oglethorpe wished to prove that everyone, even a youth, could succeed in Georgia if only he worked hard enough. His goal was to form a colony of independent yeoman farmers ready to defend their land. That is why the Trustees determined to grant land only to men. For every parcel of land, a defender.

A few weeks after abducting his little siblings from Bethesda, Milledge had the satisfaction of hearing that the staff there had been embarrassed. Milledge reported it this way:

"Mr. Barber, the guy who flogged the boy some time ago, is supposed to be an Anglican, but somehow he has become a firm believer in predestination, like the Presbyterians; and he has even converted Habersham to this dogma."

"Who's Habersham?" Margo asked.

"James Habersham. He came over with Whitefield to teach at the orphanage and has become the business manager there. The two of them tried to convert Pastor Christopher Orton to their faith, but the obstinate clergyman stood firm. They invited themselves to tea at the parsonage and insisted upon converting him to their dogma. They became so obnoxious that Orton had to call the constable; and Barber and Habersham spent the night in jail."

～

Although still inexperienced in matters of the heart, young Milledge saw that something was brewing between his servant Stout and the serving girl Margo, who constantly found excuses to pass the Milledge house when fetching wood or water for her mistress.

"Why don't you marry her?" the young master asked.

"I'm much too old for her."

"She doesn't seem to think so. I see her eyeing you all the time. Besides that, there's plenty of space for both of you in your room; and

21

she'd be a good mother to my young 'uns."

Stout pondered this for some time, afraid that all Margo felt for him was gratitude for his help on shipboard. Finally, goaded on by his young master, he made up his mind. The next time he saw Margo pass the Milledge house he walked up to her, put his hands firmly on her shoulders, looked her straight in the eye, and asked, "Will you marry me?"

Margo threw her arms around him, hugged him as tightly as she could, gave him a kiss on his cheek, and said, both laughing and crying, "I will, I will." It was the first time she had ever kissed any man but her father, and that was the only kind of kiss she knew. She then picked up her pail, took it to her mistress, asked for the evening off, and returned to Stout to make plans for the wedding.

That evening the engaged couple heard that the Reverend Henri François Chifelle of Purysburg was in town. He had traveled the twenty-five miles from that Swiss settlement on the Savannah River for a rather lucrative burial, yet he would still charge the couple for his transportation in addition to his usual high marriage fee.

"What should we do?" Stout asked. "When Pastor Boltzius comes down to Savannah from Ebenezer, some miles further up the river, he never charges for his services or his travel."

"Yes, but he also makes people post their banns three weeks in advance, so let's not wait," Margo countered.

"We could ask the Anglican minister Orton," Stout suggested. "He doesn't charge anything to perform the ceremony."

"But then we and our friends wouldn't understand it." They settled for Chifelle.

The marriage service was simple, being attended only by the Milledges, the Schneiders, and about a dozen Swiss well-wishers. Milledge lent the newlyweds his house for the wedding night by taking his family to visit Noble Jones at Wormsloe, his little fort on the Isle of Hope some eleven miles south of Savannah.

"Jones was a friend of my father on the voyage to Savannah," Milledge said, "and I played with his son Noble Wimberly on the *Anne*. That was the first ship to bring colonists to Georgia."

Augusta Schneider interpreted for Margo's benefit.

~

Knowing sex only from the barnyard, Margo was neither offended nor disappointed on her wedding night when Stout went straight to his goal, without tenderness or foreplay. I am happy being a wife, a *Hausfrau*, Frau Stout, she thought. I have a husband in place of a father, and I'll be a mother to the Milledge children.

Margo immediately took over the care of the Milledge family and did all the cooking, sewing, and laundry; and she consoled the little children when they needed consolation. By lending Stout's strong hand, Milledge compensated the Schneiders for the time Margo gave his family.

23

2

Taking Root

Stout worked all day every day clearing Milledge's fifty acres and building a fence around the property for raising hogs and keeping his cow. He was helped by the Milledge children, and by Margo whenever her mistress gave her free time.

"Come on, Hensel," Stout called one bright day to the Schneiders' little yellow mongrel with a white tip to its tail. He always took his musket with him in the remote possibility that a deer or a bear might stray across his path. While Stout was splitting rails he heard the little dog yapping fiercely. Thinking it had perhaps treed a raccoon or opossum, Stout approached with his musket in hand and found that the little dog had treed a tyger, as mountain lions were then called in Georgia.

Stout fired and the tyger fell to the ground, but only wounded. Then, when the ravening beast, as Stephens later described it, tried to attack Stout, his little dog held it at bay until its master could reload and fire another shot, this time lethal.

"Why did such a big and ferocious animal let itself be treed by such a little dog?" Margo asked when she saw the slain predator. "He could have killed it easily."

"Perhaps cats know they should run away from dogs," Stout replied, unable to think of a better answer.

Stout's young bride was immediately accepted by the Schneiders' many Dutch friends. All German-speaking people in Savannah were called indiscriminately Dutch or Palatines, regardless of whether they had come from the Germanies, Switzerland, Austria, Alsace, or any other German-speaking part of the ailing Holy Roman Empire. The inhabitants of Ebenezer were always called Salzburgers, even if they were Swiss, as a few of them really were. Only the Moravians were called Germans.

"Who are the Moravians?" Margo asked Mrs. Schneider.

"I've heard they're religious refugees from Moravia in eastern Germany," the Swiss woman replied. "They've been persecuted for centuries by the Catholic Hapsburgs. Some of them slipped across the border into the Protestant state of Saxony."

"Where's that?" Margo's knowledge of what lay outside of Canton Bern was skimpy.

"Somewhere in eastern Germany," Frau Schneider answered, not very sure herself. "Boltzius has told us all about them. They found refuge on an estate belonging to a Count von Zinzendorf, a Pietist nobleman who allowed them to found a village on his property. With Oglethorpe's help, Zinzendorf sent some of them here to Georgia, where they have distinguished themselves through their piety and industry."

"They must be the people who sang hymns all during the storm on the *Europa*," Margo suggested. "I understand they are the best workers here."

"John Wesley, our pastor, was so impressed by these devout and diligent settlers in Georgia," Mrs. Schneider continued, "that he decided to visit Herrnhut, their headquarters in Germany." Margo heard so much about the English minister that she decided he must have been the little English clergyman the Switzers met at Neus on their ill-starred journey to the Carolina paradise.

"Why did Wesley leave Georgia?" Margo asked Frau Schneider, who had been in Savannah long enough to know all the gossip.

"He was more or less run out of town by Thomas Causton, the keeper of the stores. Because of his position as storekeeper, Causton was such a powerful man that we Swiss and Germans all thought him the mayor. Wesley fell in love with Causton's niece, Sophy Hopkey, and it was assumed that they would marry, but then he dropped his suit."

"Why did he do that?" Margo asked.

"The Moravians convinced him that celibacy is a holier state than wedlock. When he withdrew his suit, the girl became angry and married William Williamson, a very important man in the town, rumored to be the illegitimate son of a high nobleman. A short time later Wesley repelled Sophy from Holy Communion on the grounds that she was not honest in her confession, and Causton and Williamson suspected he repelled her out of spite. A grand jury of fifty men was called up, but Wesley skipped town rather than show up. He left the country hurriedly and then visited the Moravians at their headquarters in Germany."

"That must be why he was in Neus," Margo suggested, remembering the odd little clergyman who had tried to dissuade them from going to Carolina. How I wish we had listened, she thought.

"John's brother Charles, Oglethorpe's secretary, was also run out of Georgia by women," Mrs. Schneider continued. "A Mrs. John Hawkins was at first his obedient pupil, but she tired of him, especially when he disapproved of her love life. She and some of her cronies made life at Frederica too unbearable for the annoying busybody."

Margo listened avidly to all this gossip. It might explain a lot about her new home.

≈

Gregarious by nature, Margo met members of all the German-speaking groups, even though her Swiss dialect sounded strange and almost incomprehensible to many of them. She also became acquainted with two German Jewish families, who had arrived in the first year of the colony along with a far greater number of Sephardic Jews from Portugal, refugees from the Inquisition.

"We Swiss and Germans," Mrs. Schneider told Margo, "do business mostly with Benjamin Sheftall of Frankfurt on the Oder because we speak the same language."

The well-informed widow continued, "Sheftall treated the first Salzburger transport, or traveling party, to a rice soup on their first morning in Savannah."

"He has helped them in many ways," the younger widow added, "for example as interpreter with the English authorities. Boltzius says the Sheftalls speak good German. By that he means the literary standard and not Yiddish.

"How about the Minises?" Margo asked.

"We do business with them, too," the older woman added. Abraham Minis always extends credit to the Salzburgers and he also supplies provisions and service to the Moravians."

~

Not long after Margo's arrival, a scandalous story spread throughout the Dutch community. A woman visiting from Frederica reported that the Anglican minister there, William Norris, had seduced a Dutch girl named Elisabetha Penner. Colonel Stephens, an ardent Anglican, was furious at such calumny.

"Give the scandal monger two hundred lashes," he commanded, "unless she recants and admits to lying." This the frightened woman readily did.

Some months later the Penner girl, pregnant, was found lost with a guide in a swamp near Ebenezer. Norris had tried to send her to Charleston, but the guide had lost his way. She told the whole sordid story to Boltzius and implored God for forgiveness.

"Why did you give yourself to that man outside the bonds of holy matrimony?" the puritanical pastor asked.

"I didn't give myself. He took me."

"Did you resist."

"With all my might."

"Did you cry out?"

"No, I was afraid to. I knew nobody would believe me."

Because she had not cried out, she was guilty, in Boltzius' Old Testament eyes, of whoredom. The civil authorities eventually believed her story and attributed the child to Norris, even though his friends had tried to put the blame on a Palatine named Jacob Ruf, or Roof as the authorities spelled his name. Unconcerned with the child's paternity, Margo did her share of tending to the infant until it died a few months later. It was not her responsibility to care for the child, but that is the way she always reacted.

~

At about this time Savannah received a human cargo as miserable as the one aboard the *Europa*. It was a shipload of Irish convicts, a term that included not only common murderers and thieves but also worthy people who had tried to resist the English rent collectors or who had spoken disrespectfully of or to their English landlords. Their ship had been driven off its course to the West Indies and had sweltered for weeks in the doldrums until all food and water had given out and many of the passengers had starved to death or died of thirst. Margo watched sympathetically as the pitiful survivors were carried ashore.

"What's going to be done with them?" she asked.

"They say," someone answered, "that Oglethorpe was so sorry for them that he bought them all."

"What's he going to do with them?"

"He's going to give them as servants to some of the worthier widows in town."

Unfortunately for some of the widows, this was no blessing. After nursing their newly acquired servants for some time, they had to bury them. Only a few widows got husbands for their efforts. Since Catholics were not tolerated in Georgia, these immigrants were all declared Protestant, as some were and others became. One of them, named Shannon, told the pastor that he wanted to convert to Protestantism, but the clergyman was astute enough to know he really just wanted a pair of shoes.

Augusta Schneider was among the widows who received an Irish deportee, hers being a farmer named Patrick O'Connor, who had thrashed his English landlord's greedy agent. Like most of the others, he was sick for a long time and was a heavy burden for his mistress. What surprised Margo most was that Patrick could hardly speak English, not nearly so well as the Schneiders.

"Why can't Patrick speak?" Stout asked. "Is he weak minded?"

"English isn't his language," Augusta explained. "He's from County Kerry in the west of Ireland. In the west the people still speak their Irish language. Most of them know just a few words of English. They are like the Highlanders down at Darien, who have a preacher who preaches in Gaelic and an officer who gives his commands in that language, too."

While helping nurse the sick convicts, Margo noticed the large number of men wearing rosaries.

"Will the Catholics be allowed to remain?" she asked an Englishman named Francis Harris, who could speak German.

"Sure," the sallow-faced merchant answered, "but not officially. There are no religious restrictions here. We have Jews, Baptists, and even Moravians. Catholics are excluded only because people are afraid they may make common cause with the Spaniards in Florida, but I don't think these poor devils here will ever be of any danger to us."

"Are there many Catholics here?" Margo asked.

"More than the Trustees think," Harris answered, taking a deep breath. "To get to America many Catholic Germans claim to be Protestant, and the Trustees have commissioned a Mr. James Horner to examine all immigrants to Georgia to see whether they are really Protestants.

"Recently," Harris continued, "a Catholic girl indentured to the Trustees left a baby on Benjamin Sheftall's doorstep before fleeing to her co-religionists at Saint Augustine. Everyone who knows that pious man knows he is not guilty, yet Boltzius still believes the Jew is the father. Perhaps he is annoyed because Sheftall has not yet converted to the Christian faith, as the preacher was so sure he would."

"Why did he think that?" Margo asked.

"Because he gave Sheftall some Yiddish religious books by Johann Callenberg, a missionary to the Jews. Pastor Quincy, our first minister, was right when he said that Sheftall's kindness to the Salzburgers did'nt mean that he wished to change religions. He helped them just because of his generous disposition." Margo decided right then to call on the Sheftalls.

～

"Have you seen the picture of Whitefield's orphanage?" Augusta Schneider asked Margo one morning.

"Not yet. Where is it?"

"I saw it at Colonel Stephens' house when delivering his starched shirts this morning. It's the frontispiece of Whitefield's printed account book in which he lists all donations to and expenditures for the orphanage."

"Who drew it?"

"Noble Jones. And this time he put his initials on it."

"Why *this time*?"

"I guess he's learned his lesson. When Savannah was only a year

29

old he made a view of the town and let the upholsterer Peter Gordon take it to the Trustees for him. They thought Gordon had drawn it, so they had it engraved under his name. Gordon never claimed he had drawn it, but he did keep the £ 7 reward. Hearing wrongly that the reward was £ 100, Jones was very angry at the 'infringement on his rights', as he called it."

~

Early one morning Augusta Schneider saw a line of men waiting at Colonel Stephens' office. They were mostly German and Swiss redemptioners. She asked the last man in line,

"What's everyone waiting for?"

"To get a farm at Vernonburg."

"Where's that?"

"A new village on the Vernon River about ten miles south of here. A lot of us are now finishing our indentures, and the British officials are trying to keep us in Georgia by giving us farms, livestock, and provisions for a year."

Since her indenture was almost finished, Augusta joined the line. When she reached its head, Colonel Stephens had to tell her that Georgia followed the law of tail-male.

"What's that?" Augusta asked.

"That means only men can hold land in Georgia," the colonel explained, with a very apologetic tone of voice. "Every parcel of land should be defended by a man. No woman can inherit or hold land, but her son can if he's of age."

"What do the people here think of the law?"

"They don't like it," the colonel admitted, "and neither do I, but I have to enforce the Trustees' decisions. I hear that some people have even left the colony because of the law."

Pleased at what he saw on his second visit to Vernonburg, Stephens exclaimed, "It's amazing how much harder the indentured servants work after gaining their freedom and working for themselves. They do as much now in an hour as they used to do in a whole day."

Margo agreed. She had never seen anyone in Switzerland work so poorly as most of the indentured servants in Georgia did. They wouldn't

30

have kept their job for one day in the old country.

Sixty 'long lots' were cleared in the first year, and a year later the colonel walked through a mile of unbroken wheat fields. In his crop reports to the Trustees he put Vernonburg as second only to Ebenezer in the quantity of crops produced.

~

Despite their strenuous farm work, some of the younger unmarried settlers at Acton and Vernonburg continued spending Saturday nights in Savannah carousing in the pub. One night, to avoid the long walk home, several of them borrowed the horses tied in front of the pub and rode home on them, turning them loose there to find their way back. Unfortunately, some of the horses could not find their way home and strayed around for days, to the distress of their owners.

"I understand that several of the thieves were recognized and arrested," Augusta Schneider said to Stout.

"Quite so. Colonel Stephens sentenced them to the stocks and fifty lashes."

Hearing this, Margo went to their aid with the help of Sheftall as interpreter. Despite her timidity and awe before a man of such authority as Stephens, she pleaded, "Your Honor, these men did not steal the horses, they just borrowed them and thought they would go straight home. It was not a theft, but simply a boyish prank, which they would not have committed if sober. In view of the excellent progress they're making on their farms you should not whip them."

Moved by her plea, the benign old gentleman canceled the whipping but let the malefactors sit a few hours in the stocks.

Another unruly Palatine servant was not so lucky. Because some of the indentured servants were sulky and refused to work on holy days, Stephens thought it a wise precaution to forbid them to carry arms, as most of them did. When the storekeeper Thomas Causton saw one of his servants hunting, he called on the constable John Fallowfield to disarm the lawbreaker. This the constable could do only by striking him on his head several times with the grip of his leather riding crop. The unruly man was then put in the brig. The next day the surly servant was found dead in a pool of vomit. Fallowfield and the storekeeper, backed by the coroner and the Salzburgers' physician, testified that the man had choked to death in his own vomit, but the man's wife and most of the other Dutch attributed the death to the beating.

"He should have submitted to arrest peacefully," Stout muttered softly, being sure none of his countrymen heard him.

~

The Stouts' marriage was running smoothly when a talebearer arrived from Germany and reported that Johann Staud had a wife and several children back in Saarbruecken. Colonel Stephens summoned Stout at once.

"Is it true that you have a wife in Germany?"

"No, Sir. I had one but no longer have," the heavy-set farmer answered.

"Did she die?"

"No, Sir. She deserted me. When I had to come to America, she refused to come with me; and I consider that desertion."

"Why did you have to come to America?"

"My wife had eaten me out of house and home. She was the daughter of a tradesman and knew nothing about farming and would not learn in order to help me. Then, to make matters worse, she invited her three brothers to stay with us, and they did no work but ran up debts against my farm. The creditors finally took over the farm, and I shared the remaining money with my wife before leaving for Georgia with only a few thalers in my pocket."

Colonel Stephens seemed satisfied with this excuse and changed Stout's legal status from single to divorced and remarried. Despite this unwelcome news from Germany, Margo continued to live with Stout, with no offense to Milledge or to the Dutch community. Colonel Stephens did not object to this union, being well aware that most of the British officials in Savannah lived with their "housekeepers". Being an elderly gentleman, Stephens had only a housekeeper. He did not need a "housekeeper".

The Stouts' questionable marriage might well have lasted had it not come to the attention of Pastor Boltzius during one of his monthly visits to Savannah for preaching the gospel and administering Holy Communion to the German-speaking residents.

"We cannot allow such an irregularity," the preacher told his assistant, Israel Gronau, a gangling young man five years younger than his superior and ten inches taller. "It would reflect badly on the good name of the Dutch in Savannah and, indirectly, on our Salzburgers. It might even turn away some of our donors."

On every visit to Savannah, Boltzius called on Margo, the great sinner, and threatened her with the wrath of God if she would not cease her bigamous relationship. Also, he repelled her from Holy Communion, which was tantamount to excommunication.

Finally bowing to pressure, Margo left Stout's bed and returned to her room at the widow Schneiders' house. In her bed she missed the warmth and security she had felt in Stout's strong arms and the pleasure she felt in satisfying him.

3

Ebenezer Exile

On his difficult and dangerous visits to Savannah, Boltzius was accompanied by Gabriel Bach, one of his parishioners, who was immediately attracted to the now single woman. Like everyone else, Margo was taken by the ex-cavalryman's colorful uniform, his broad shoulders, and flaxen hair. Gabriel was not a true Salzburger, he had joined the second Salzburger transport four years earlier at Memmingen in southern Germany.

"I am a Protestant," Gabriel had declared. "I wish to go to Georgia because there aren't any Catholics there to persecute me." Most of the Salzburgers suspected that he was actually a Catholic, even if a lapsed one, who just wanted free passage to America.

"We cannot deny," one of them admitted, "that he knows the Augsburg Confession better than any of us."

Gabriel could read, more or less, and he realized that it would be useful to know something of the Lutheran articles of faith if he were to pass as a Protestant. He never missed an opportunity to discuss theology with Evangelical preachers along the way. Accepted as a Salzburger, he did not have to submit to James Horner's examination.

Gabriel was a born horseman. His father had been equerry to a petty count in Bavaria; and he had grown up riding and training horses. At age sixteen he ran away and enlisted in a Bavarian hussar troop serving the Holy Roman Empire. His first tour of duty consisted of putting down the rebellion of the Archbishop of Salzburg's mutinous and murderous peasants.

"It didn't take me long," he later assured Pastor Boltzius, "to see that the alleged bloodthirsty insurgents were really peaceful Christian souls. They just wanted the right to continue practicing their Protestant religion, which they had been practicing since the time of Luther. In escorting these wretched dissidents to the border and exile, I did as much as I could to comfort them. I even attended some of their prayer meetings and was greatly edified."

Disheartened by the hateful campaign in Salzburg, Gabriel left the Bavarian service and went to Vienna, where he easily found work as a groom in the Spanish Riding School, the Imperial riding academy. There he helped train the famous Lippizaner stallions, standing for hours holding the young horses on the longe, at the end of which they walked, trotted, or galloped in a circle around the trainer while obeying his commands.

"Well done!" the Riding Master shouted upon seeing Gabriel put his horses through their paces. "Next week you can start training the stallions in their passage, piaffe, and capriole."

Gabriel's career seemed promising until the Riding Master's daughter accused him of making her pregnant. Innocent and not wishing to acknowledge paternity of another man's child, he quietly disappeared.

Gabriel next returned to the count's stables and steadily gained favor with the count until a jealous forester reported seeing the ex-cavalryman poaching in his lord's game preserve. To avoid arrest, Gabriel fled with his horse to Augsburg, where he learned that a second Salzburger transport was soon to leave Memmingen for Georgia. Catching up with them at that south German city, he sold the count's horse, bridle, saddle, and accoutrements but kept his kepi, compass, and field glass.

Gabriel told the exiles his sad tale of religious persecution, which Jean Vat, the Salzburgers' Swiss commissioner, accepted at face value. He marched with the Salzburgers cross-country along the "Romantic Way" to the Main and sailed down the Main and the Rhine to Rotterdam, receiving his share of the food and alms given to the religious exiles in all the Protestant villages they went through. Gabriel won the Salzburgers' affection in a Catholic town by drawing his sword and chasing away some drunks who were throwing stones at the heretics.

The trip to Dover and London was uneventful, as was the tedious voyage across the Atlantic on the *Prince of Wales*.

～

By the time Gabriel reached Georgia with the second Salzburger transport, the land at Ebenezer chosen for the first Salzburgers had proved not only infertile but also inaccessible.

"It was stupid," one of the more outspoken Salzburgers complained, "to put us on Ebenezer Creek." Anton Rieser was the first to see how poor the spot was, and he was the only one who had the courage to question God's (i.e., Oglethorpe's) choice of a site for the Salzburgers.

"What's wrong with this place?" Gabriel asked.

"Ebenezer Creek's blocked by logs and cypress tree roots. Jonas and Baron von Reck tried for over a week to bring their rowboat up here from the Savannah River, but they never made it."

The Salzburgers confused the name Jones with that of Jonas, the man swallowed by the whale. Noble Jones had surveyed Ebenezer, and von Reck had led the first Salzburger transport.

Even Boltzius eventually saw the folly of their location. In a secret confrontation with Oglethorpe, he held his ground. "The Salzburgers will perish unless the location of their settlement is changed," he argued.

"If you are really sure of that," Oglethorpe acquiesced, "you may move." Deep down in his heart he knew he had placed the Salzburgers where he did for strategic rather than for economic reasons. The surviving inhabitants were then removed to the Red Bluff at the mouth of Ebenezer Creek on the navigable Savannah River, where Jones surveyed and planned an elaborate city for them. The Salzburgers took the name Ebenezer with them, thus giving the illusion of continuity.

"I discovered fertile soil on the Red Bluff," Rieser boasted, "while gathering acorns for my swine. Now Ebenezer is the new town on the Red Bluff. The older site is called Old Ebenezer and serves the Trustees as a cowpen, or cattle ranch."

~

Being an expert horseman, Gabriel chose to serve as scout, courier, and hunter rather than to establish a farm as the other settlers of the new Ebenezer wished to do. He also served as cowboy in finding and bringing in the Salzburgers' straying cattle. "Why do you people let your cattle range?" Gabriel asked Rieser, who already had eight head of cattle.

"Don't you lose a lot of them to rustlers and Indians?"

"We do indeed," Rieser admitted. "When we first came here, we employed herdsmen to keep the cows together. Oglethorpe and other people praised us for not letting the cattle run wild as the other Georgians did. But we learned that it is actually easier to let them roam at will."

"Why's that?"

"The cattle thrive best in the canebrakes, where the reeds are far more fattening than the wire grass and sedgebrush in the pine barrens. The trouble is that it's too hard for the herdsmen to follow them in the swamps. We finally realized that the English cattlemen were wise to let the cattle range."

"But don't the unguarded cows stray into other people's gardens and fields?"

"That's their right. We have the custom of 'fence out'. That means, if you don't want other people's cattle on your crops, you have to fence them out. Each of us Salzburgers has his own branding iron, which is registered down in Savannah. When we round up the cows to brand their calves, we know which are our cows and therefore which are our calves. The men at the English cowpen at Old Ebenezer brand a lot of calves belonging to our cows, and we lose a lot of cows to Indians, who shoot them just for their bells."

Boltzius disapproved of Gabriel's unstable life, yet he judged him the best qualified man to protect him on his travels. He was especially reassured by Kumpan, Gabriel's well-trained hound, who circled them en route just out of musket range, thus making it unlikely that any Indians could ambush them.

"Kumpan must be a mixture of breeds," the pastor remarked.

"Probably including great dane, wolfhound, and mastiff," Gabriel agreed.

"He's larger than any other hound I've seen in Georgia," the pastor continued, "and gentler than most."

When going to Savannah, the two men and their canine guardian usually rode to Abercorn, a defunct Scots settlement on the Savannah, from which they could reach the city by rowboat with the ebb tide in a matter of hours. They always returned with a flood tide, which brought them up as far as Purysburg, so they only had to row a few miles from there to Abercorn. A pious Englishman, the only resident left at Abercorn, kept and fed their horses for them and furnished them lodgings when requested.

After Margo had left Stout's bed, Gabriel called on her whenever he could elude Boltzius on their visits to Savannah. Or he could visit her secretly by pretending to carry messages for Colonel Stephens to Fort Argyle, a small fortress on the Great Ogeechee River some twenty miles south of Ebenezer. Gabriel was smitten by Margo's oval face, her finely chiseled features, and her full and sensuous lips. He desired her more than he had ever desired any other woman. She must love me too, he decided, because she visibly quivers if I touch her, even if accidentally.

Whenever Gabriel looked at Margo, she felt a stirring of yearnings she did not know she could feel. Even while she was trying to look Boltzius in the eye, her gaze was irresistibly drawn to Gabriel's steel grey orbs, as grey as the blade of his saber, which he often whetted when they were sitting together. Gabriel had a peculiar mannerism. When he looked anyone in the eyes, his face was always turned a bit askew. It was almost as if he had received the order "Eyes Right." Does he do that on purpose? Margo asked herself. Does he want to show off his handsome profile? In any case, turning his head like that is very attractive, even if a bit flirtatious.

One evening Gabriel found Margo at the Wizenbakers, as the British authorities had renamed the Weissenbachers, and paid attention only to her. Although still grief-stricken at the loss of her family, Margo could sometimes forget her sorrow momentarily when surrounded by joyful people. While the young folk were dancing polkas to the music of a dulcimer and a flute, she especially enjoyed dancing with the broad shouldered cavalryman, who held her tightly in his muscular arms as if she were weightless. As the guests began departing, the handsome trooper approached Margo, hat in hand.

"May I have the honor of escorting you home?" he asked in his gallant style, knowing that the Schneiders were spending the night in Vernonburg.

"Yes, I shall be highly honored," Margo answered in a courtly manner, the way the ladies in the Gilded Coach would have answered.

Upon reaching her doorstep, Gabriel drew her close for a goodnight kiss and sensed her inner turmoil. First, he kissed her on her forehead and cheeks, while caressing her back through her summer smock. Then he gave her a probing kiss on her lips, sensual yet tender; and she could feel his heart pounding like a barley stamp.

When Gabriel finally gave her a full and firm kiss on her unresisting mouth, Margo felt a bolt of searing pleasure course through her whole body. She parted her lips and no longer tried to push him away, knowing that her legs had gone limp and would not support her. Nor did she resist when he lifted her up, carried her to her bed, and began to undress her.

But then the dream was shattered. The voices of the Schneider women were approaching the front door. They had changed their plans and postponed their visit until the next day. Gabriel gave Margo an affectionate kiss, threw a blanket over her, and climbed quietly out the back window.

Margo was astonished at, and ashamed of, her quick surrender, for she knew she would not have opposed Gabriel's advances, or even wished to oppose them. What power did he have over her? Physical attraction was often attributed to magic. People said a person was charming, bewitching, enchanting, fascinating, or spellbinding or had cast a love spell. But in all these cases the spellbinder was a woman, not a man.

After her violent reaction to Gabriel's kiss, she speculated as to whether he had indeed cast a spell on her. In any case, she would never risk being alone with him again. No, never! Her sudden aloofness was keenly disappointing for Gabriel, who had at last found a woman who truly met his physical needs. His chaperoned visits with Margo were most unrewarding and aroused desires he had never felt before. None of his previous affairs had had this effect.

~

Gabriel had not intended to marry, at least not for many years, yet he finally resolved to do so if there was no other way to win his beloved, who dominated his thoughts both night and day. On his next journey with Boltzius he said, "Pastor Boltzius, I wish to marry Margaret Staud."

That put Boltzius on the horns of a dilemma. He did not approve of fallen women, nor did he wish any scandal to tarnish the good name of his congregation.

"I don't think you should marry her. She is guilty of bigamy."

"But she didn't know Staud was married," the eager suitor countered.

"Yes, but she did not leave him when she was told."

"She has now done so. I thought you preached that a sinner can be forgiven if he repents his sin. In our congregation there are several girls and women named Maria Magdalena after that sinful but penitent and forgiven woman."

Boltzius reluctantly agreed to the marriage, but only if the great sinner would do church penance first. Margo agreed to this condition, and the young couple moved up to Ebenezer, where she was lodged at the orphanage and where he retained his quarters with bachelor friends. The Ebenezer orphanage, the first in the thirteen colonies, was more than an orphanage, it was the nerve center of the community.

"This orphanage," Mrs. Boltzius told the young couple, "is modeled on the Orphanage at Halle, where my husband and Pastor Gronau were teachers."

"Where's Halle?" Margo asked.

"In Saxony, somewhere in eastern Germany," Mrs. Boltzius answered. "There are three married couples in the house, but just a few children. The building serves as a hospital, guest house, and store house; and we also use it for making silk and for many other purposes."

"I heard this orphanage was Whitefield's chief inspiration for building his own at Bethesda," Gabriel said.

Margo's main function at the orphanage was milking the cows, of which the orphanage owned many despite the "black water", a disease that was destroying many cattle in Savannah and Vernonburg.

"Why do all the cows want to be milked by Margo?" a milkmaid named Veronica asked enviously. "As soon as the cowherd brings them back from pasture, they all head straight for her." No one could account for this bovine preference.

Margo introduced several new ways of making curds, whey, and clabber, methods common in Switzerland but perhaps not in Salzburg. She also reeled silk for her hosts. She enjoyed reeling silk, but she hated working with the worms, which stank dreadfully when they died. The Trustees invested much capital in developing a silk industry in Georgia so England would not have to import so much silk from France and Italy.

In Switzerland Margo had contributed to the family income by spinning both wool and flax. Prior to her stay in Ebenezer, Boltzius had bought some sheep and also some flax seed, both of which flourished, so there was always spinning to be done.

Although the Salzburger women were courteous to her, Margo felt shunned as a sinner. The only person who seemed entirely frank with her was Barbara Maurer, a young woman who had come alone with the second transport. Curious to know why this one woman sought her out, she asked Veronica about her.

"One evening when Barbara was delivering the laundry to a young single man named Hans Zittrauer, she stayed too long in his room. Some old folks across the street noticed this indiscretion and reported it to Boltzius. Boltzius summoned the young couple, and they solemnly denied any wrongdoing. They even swore a holy oath in church that they were innocent."

"Was the matter dropped?" Margo asked.

"For a while the matter was relegated to oblivion. Those were Boltzius' very words, and we were told never to mention it again."

"And then?"

"Boltzius happened to give a fire-and-brimstone sermon, something he almost never does. For him, the greatest punishment after death is to be unable to go to heaven and thus never see one's loved ones again. Usually he does not mention hell, but this time he did, and most gruesomely. Barbara became terrified and confessed to everything, and she and Zittrauer had to do church penance."

41

One afternoon, while Margo was reeling silk in the orphanage, a tall Indian brave wearing only a breech-cloth entered uninvited. She cowered, too terrified to cry out. The Indian ignored her, picked up an axe, felt its cutting edge, and then returned it to its place. Next he went into the kitchen and returned with a loaf of bread and a thick slice of ham. He departed without a word of thanks.

"Pastor Boltzius, Pastor Boltzius," Margo shouted, running to the nearby parsonage.

"What is it, my child?" the minister asked. Margo was taken aback. She had never seen that man of God so informal. His white wig of authority was lying on the table and he was smoking a pipe. His brown hair was close-cropped, with a bit of gray showing at the temples. Hiding her embarrassment, Margo answered,

"An Indian. He came right in and took some bread and ham."

"You'll just have to put up with it," the pastor commiserated, putting down his pipe. "The Indians don't exactly understand our ideas of private property. They share and share alike, and they expect us to do the same. That makes it difficult for the Salzburgers, because the Indians make many demands but usually have nothing with them to give in exchange. Also, they are 'Indian givers'."

"What does that mean?"

"If they give or sell you something, they are free to return any time and demand it back. That's why I try to discourage my congregation from doing business with them, in accordance with the Trustees' wise command."

"Just look at that!" Margo exclaimed, pointing to her recent uninvited guest's squaw. "The poor woman's carrying a papoose. All the family's belongings are piled up on her, while her husband isn't carrying a thing."

Margo received much more chivalrous treatment from Gabriel. He was of humble origins, but at the Riding School in Vienna he had observed the behavior of the lords and ladies who rode there. The young gentleman always walked beside his lady, opened doors for her, carried her luggage, and minded his language in her presence. Gabriel acted similarly on those rare occasions he was able to be with Margo.

Some weeks later a small party of Choctaws was camping nearby. A young Creek brave who came to Ebenezer to sell honey recognized the Choctaw who had killed his father some years earlier. Taking careful aim, he shot the offender dead, thus restoring his own besmirched honor. He then reloaded his musket and handed it to his chief, who accepted it ceremoniously and executed him with it. This made reprisal by the other tribe unnecessary, and thus the long-lasting point of honor had been amicably resolved. Margo, who was standing close to the victim, was shocked. She did not know that her own ancestors a thousand years earlier would have reacted in the same way.

~

"We are irked not only by uninvited Indians," Boltzius sighed, "but also by the Trustees' indentured servants at the cowpen at Old Ebenezer. Especially by two young Swiss rascals named Wilhelm Taescher and Heinrich Meyer. One Sunday, while the congregation was singing with great fervor, Taescher and Meyer arrived disgustingly drunk and sang parodies of the Salzburgers' hymns. When I asked them to leave, they behaved impudently and let me know what they thought of preachers."

Boltzius was incensed at such an outrage. His authority had never been questioned. He summoned the newly appointed constable, Thomas Bichler.

"Take Gabriel with you and arrest the two miscreants for their blasphemy. We cannot put up with such behavior."

"Very well, Sir."

Before the two lawmen reached Old Ebenezer, Meyer fled and went up the Savannah River, where he killed an Indian in a drunken brawl. Taescher submitted to arrest and was taken down to Savannah for punishment. When Colonel Stephens heard the case, he scolded the disrespectful young man and made him promise never to annoy Boltzius again, but he did not punish him. Boltzius was left with the expense of the rowers to and from Savannah.

A week later Taescher returned to Ebenezer while almost everyone else was at church and "debauched" Meyer's sister, Magdalena, an indentured servant, "under her mother's roof," as Boltzius reported the outrage. Some time later Magdalena disappeared. Taescher had taken her away and married her. By now he was known by the name of Dasher.

∽

"That's a fantastic sawmill," Margo said upon seeing the water-powered one the Salzburgers had recently built. "I hear it's the first successful one in all Georgia."

"That it is, to be sure," the proud master-carpenter George Kogler agreed. "The hardware was donated by the Trustees, whose sawmill at Old Ebenezer was destroyed by a flood before completion." All the work at New Ebenezer had been directed by Kogler, who had previously built Jerusalem Church as well as the orphanage.

"The mill was designed," Kogler continued, "by an English engineer named Joseph Avery, who died soon after beginning the project. Fortunately, he left such good diagrams that I could finish the mill myself."

"Just see how the four big saws rip right through the thick tree trunks," Margo remarked. "The mill is doing the work of sixty men, to judge by what work I've seen done by hand in Savannah."

"You must be right," Kogler agreed with evident satisfaction.

"Down there in Savannah," Margo continued, "one man stands on the trunk while the other stands in a pit under it, jointly pulling and pushing a large hand saw. I've heard that this new sawmill uses the same millrace that was made for the earlier gristmill." Margo tried to learn everything she could about her new home.

Most remarkable were the prefabricated houses Kogler was then producing. After making a satisfactory model, he cut and numbered several copies of each piece, complete with dowels and mortised joints. These could then be assembled quickly with the aid of written directions. The market for prefabricated houses was mostly in the West Indies, where forests had given way to sugar cane fields.

∽

Gabriel was ill at ease in the godly atmosphere reigning among the

44

Salzburgers, but he willingly put up with it for the three weeks his banns were being proclaimed in Savannah and Purysburg. Like Margo, whom he saw seldom and never alone, he well earned his keep. His chief service was finding the Salzburgers' straying cattle to brand them.

"Mr. Barker," he told the English cattle keeper at Old Ebenezer, "your underlings are illegally branding the Salzburgers' still unbranded calves." Because of his military posture and command presence, Gabriel could deal with the devious Barker better than the peaceful Salzburgers could even though his English was still sadly wanting.

"I'm sorry if that's so," Barker apologized, hoping the Trustees would not hear about his cattle branding and rustling. "I'll try to keep an eye on my men."

Gabriel also endeared himself to the Salzburgers by shooting and killing a bear that was blamed for the death of several calves. "The credit should go to Kumpan," he suggested. "After all, he was the one who treed the beast."

～

While Gabriel and Margo were still at Ebenezer, Oglethorpe stopped by on his way from the back country to meet a party of Chickasaws at Mary Musgrove's cowpen.

"Who's Mary Musgrove?" Gabriel asked Mrs. Boltzius, who was carrying a large hamper of mulberry leaves for her silk worms.

"Mary is the daughter of a Scots trader and a Tuckabatchee woman," the pastor's wife answered. "She frequently serves Oglethorpe as interpreter; and she also owns a large plantation and trading house near here on Pipemaker Creek. She often entertains Indian warriors for Oglethorpe."

Despite his important business with the Indians, Oglethorpe found time on this short visit to have two large millstones brought up from Savannah for the new gristmill the Salzburgers were building.

"How can Oglethorpe find so much time for his people?" Margo asked. "Did you notice that he treats the pastors as his equals and knows the names of many of the Salzburgers? They say he never rests."

～

45

When Gabriel learned the details of the church penance demanded of his fiancée, he was highly incensed.

"I won't have my wife humiliated like that in public," he swore. "We could never live at Ebenezer after that. She would be spurned just like Barbara Maurer."

Instead, Gabriel galloped down to Fort Argyle and enlisted as a King's Ranger, a job that paid enough to support a wife. It was a perilous calling. One of the Rangers had just been ambushed and killed by transient Indians. The deceased had left a furnished hut, of which Gabriel took immediate possession.

Returning to Ebenezer for his bride, Gabriel discovered she had completed her penance and been forgiven and that they could now settle in Ebenezer if they so desired.

"It's too late now, Margo, because I've accepted the King's shilling and drunk the King's grog."

"But surely Boltzius could get you off," the worried woman pleaded. "He redeemed the convert Gottlieb Christ, who had foolishly enlisted."

"Sure," the determined Ranger answered, "but Gottlieb was consumptive. When the recruiter found that out, he didn't really want him. I don't wish to live in Ebenezer. I don't like the high-handed way Boltzius treated you."

Instead, Gabriel took his fiancée across and down the river to Purysburg to be married by the greedy Pastor Chifelle, who again charged a high fee but could not demand transportation. Among those attending their wedding was the interpreter Mary Musgrove. Although her husband John Musgrove had died and Mary had later married a Capt. Jacob Mathews, people continued to call her Mary Musgrove. Mary invited the newlyweds to spend their honeymoon at her nearby plantation, where there were some Indians and traders and much reveling and bacchanalian dancing.

"Even I can see why Boltzius won't let his pious parishioners visit such a den of iniquity." Gabriel was seldom so judgmental.

～

"Why don't you spend your wedding night in one of my storehouses?"

Mary suggested, "no one is using 'em now. There's a bedroom in each of them."

"Many thanks."

Kumpan was banished to another room. The wedding night was even more than Margo had hoped for. Although married to Stout for many months and nearly seduced by Gabriel, she was, emotionally, still an innocent. Gabriel, to the contrary, had enjoyed many amorous adventures during his military career, sometimes with experienced women who could teach him the niceties of love-making. Also, to escape boredom, he had often read erotic chapbooks, or little romances, usually badly translated into German from the original French.

Gabriel began his courtship slowly, saying the right things and showing no hurry. He even stepped into the next room to undress and put on his nightshirt and to give Margo time to do the same. Returning to their bridal chamber, he slipped under the covers with her, loosened her tight chignon, and let her glossy black hair tumble down over the snowy sheen of her candle-lit shoulders. First he kissed his love on her cheeks and the nape of her neck tenderly, while gently caressing her full breasts through her shift. Then he kissed her throat hungrily before placing his lips firmly on hers. Margo could hold back no longer, she surrendered to him totally. She pulled off her shift and helped him remove his nightshirt.

Had an ill wind lifted her skirt up that afternoon and let some stranger see her knee, she would have blushed crimson, but now she was completely naked yet as unashamed as Adam and Eve in the Garden before they ate the apple. Only then did she understand the saying, *Die Liebe kennt keine Scham*, "Love knows no shame."

Margo pondered the matter and asked herself how a modest maid could so willingly expose her nakedness and become a shameless sexual partner. Such introspection was something new to her.

On their second night, Margo was determined to play a more demure and feminine role and let Gabriel plead for her favors before granting them. They were sitting, fully clothed, opposite each other on two chests idly chatting when he stood up and took one of her hands in his and kissed it. In his amours he had made a discovery. If he dropped his

47

eyelids to half-mast and looked straight into a girl's eyes and stared through her, or at least through her clothing, her resistance would soon melt.

Margo was no exception. Gabriel's gaze unsettled her, she lost her resolve and jumped up and embraced him. Her breathing came in short shallow gasps as his lips wrought havoc with her senses and shattered her defenses. Then, impatient while he fumbled with the ribbons on her bodice, she finished the task herself and helped him unbutton his tunic.

4

Fort Argyle

Three days later the Ranger, his wife, his horse, and his hound reached Fort Argyle on the right bank of the Great Ogeechee.

"Do you see how black the water is?" Gabriel asked. "Now look at this." Taking a piece of white paper from his pack, he put it under the water, which made it look rusty brown. He then took a glass full of the same water and held it to the light, and the water looked clear.

"In Europe," the Ranger continued, "people travel miles to bathe in such water, which is called *Mohrwasser* or swamp water. It's supposed to cure rheumatism and almost everything else. Here we have it free. When this country gets populated, perhaps we should open a spa."

While Gabriel was talking, Margo was watching a peculiar little fish the size and shape of a pencil lying at the surface of the water.

"What do they call this fish," she asked, pointing.

"The English call it a garfish. I think that means a spear fish."

"It looks a bit like the pickerel the monks at Frauenstein put in their carp pond to keep the carp in motion," Margo said, recalling a visit to a monastery, "but a bit thinner and with a longer snout." While she was pointing at the fish, it suddenly disappeared. Almost simultaneously it reappeared several yards away. Margo had seen no sign of motion, not even a ripple.

~

Fort Argyle was not much of a fort. Margo saw only a small stockade, about a hundred feet square, surrounded by a palisade fence some eleven feet high mounted on a low embankment. On each corner stood a little wooden tower mounting a small cannon. This sufficed to stop canoes from passing the fort by day, for the fort was on a right-angle bend in the river which afforded a clear view both up and downstream. In the fort were quarters for a score of men and stalls for an equal number of horses.

When Gabriel reported to his commanding officer, or Quartermaster as he was called for unknown reasons, Margo burst out,

"Why, it's my old friend John Milledge! He's the one who rescued his brother and sister from Whitefield's orphanage. Gabriel, meet my old friend."

"Pleased to meet you, Sir. I've heard a lot about you, Sir."

"Don't bother with all the 'Sirs' except in line of duty."

"You seem awfully young to be a captain, Sir," Gabriel commented.

"It helps to be friends with Oglethorpe," the modest young officer said. "He liked my father. They came over together on the *Anne*."

Margo looked around. "Where are Richard and Frances?" she asked, shading her eyes from the sun.

"They 're with their stepmother fishing," Milledge replied.

"Stepmother?"

"Well, technically she's their sister-in-law," Milledge explained, but she's playing the role of stepmother, and doing a fine job. It's going to be confusing in a few months when she has her baby and my little sister and brother will be its aunt and uncle." Margo was delighted to see the children who had meant so much to her in Savannah. They had grown a lot, but they had not forgotten Aunt Margo.

"I'm almost jealous of your wife, because I felt myself the children's stepmother while I was working for the Schneiders." Milledge saw to it that Gabriel got the best available billets, much better than the hut he had picked out. Unlike the other cabins, this one had a boarded floor, much easier to keep clean than the dirt ones. As in the other cabins, the windows had no panes.

"If you close the heavy shutters against the rain or cold," Margo said, "the cabin is entirely dark. But I think I know a cure for it."

"And what's that?" Gabriel asked.

"I watched a squaw near Ebenezer scrape a deer hide so thin you could almost see through it. Get me a deer skin and I'll show you."

Soon afterwards Gabriel returned with a stinking deer hide and Margo began the laborious task of scraping on both sides until it was paper thin and very translucent. Gabriel mounted it in a wooden frame so that it could be removed in clement weather.

"I just hate the leather hinges on the door," Margo complained, "because you have to lift the heavy door every time you open or shut it."

Margo persuaded Gabriel to give his next deer hide to Wilhelm Mueller, the talented artisan in Ebenezer, in exchange for a pair of iron hinges. These new hinges were a great improvement because they kept the door from dragging on the floor when being opened or closed. Also, rather than sleep on the floor, Margo asked a neighbor to build her a wooden bed frame, which she then furnished with a hempen rope grid and a mattress stuffed with Spanish moss. To kill the chiggers, she smoked the moss with sulphur smoke.

~

Margo enjoyed talking to the Rangers' wives, who spoke a peculiar mixture of a half-dozen languages, including English, Welsh, Lowland Scots, Highland and Irish Gaelic, several German dialects, and even Czech. Having much time and no children, she was generous with her help. When Mrs. McDonald had her fourth child with almost no pain, Margo did not claim credit even though it was she who had put the ax under the bed to cut the birth pains. When Travis' injured hand began to fester, Margo cured it by filling the wound with spider webs.

Milledge had requested and received a grant for a gentleman's lot of five hundred acres for himself because he expected the region to develop. As soon as Margo was established in her small quarters, she asked Milledge,

"May I have some land for a garden?"

"Certainly, take as much as you want anywhere east of the fort. I'll show you a spot that's already cleared."

Someone had planted a garden there but had given up in disgust because nothing ripened. Margo saw at once that the garden was too shaded by the tall trees surrounding it.

"Can we cut down the trees that are shading the garden?" Margo asked her husband.

"Not hardly," Gabriel answered. "There are too many of them. Perhaps we should just ring them as the Salzburgers do." He showed her how to cut deep grooves through the bark around the trees so that they would die and shed their leaves and needles, thereby letting the sunlight through. Later, when timber was needed, the leafless trees could be felled, the trunk sawed into boards, and the dry branches used as firewood.

Wire grass formed a thick mat of roots over the abandoned field, roots so tough that no hoe could chop through them. Margo hired one of the men at the fort to plow up the wire grass with his ox, which had to strain mightily to break up the dense sod. There was also some crab grass, which produced rather poor forage. Boltzius, who had learned the word "crab grass" from his Salzburger parishioners, first called the weed "crop grass," thinking it came up with a crop. Later he changed the word to "grab grass," thinking it had to be grabbed, and lastly he called it "crab grass," the word "crab" being understood as "cancer" because of the way it spread.

Through much hard work Margo eventually produced fine yields of cabbages, sweet potatoes, onions, pumkins, squash, okra, kidney beans, and melons. As Boltzius had observed, the cabbages did not form heads, they just produced an abundance of leaves, which were excellent for making sauerkraut. Like Boltzius, Margo considered watermelons a true gift of God. If only my father had owned flat fertile ground like this! Franz had struggled so bravely with his steep and worn-out fields.

Margo applied a generous amount of horse manure, which was free for the taking at the stables. The manure, diluted, also nourished her vegetable and herb garden as well as her Cherokee rose bushes, of which she had many. She naturally assumed that the roses were a native plant, but Mrs. Milledge informed her that they had been imported from somewhere by the Spaniards at St. Augustine and that the Cherokees had taken seeds and planted them all around, probably for medicinal purposes, since in general they were not especially fond of flowers.

One day Hugh Bryan, a very religious planter from South Carolina, passed by Fort Argyle with a large herd of cattle he was driving to Frederica with black cowboys. Margo bought a young cow and calf with her meager savings and sold the calf for the price of both just as soon as it was weaned. The cow, Liesel, was very productive for her time, giving almost two gallons of milk every day. Margo sold enough milk, butter, and cheese to buy all the food she needed. Since Gabriel brought home much venison and other game, little of his pay was spent on food.

Time went on its way, and Margo became used to life as farmwife. In time she felt very much at home. The winter had been mild, and she had enjoyed the absence of gnats and mosquitoes, but now that spring was approaching, the pests began to appear again. At least the swallows appeared, too. Margo watched their graceful flight and thanked the Lord that they were devouring so many insects. As the evening darkened, the swallows and whipoorwills were gradually replaced by bats, whose jerky flights were equally beneficial.

~

Early one bright spring morning Gabriel saw Margo putting a bowl of milk under the front stoop.

"What's that for?" he asked, pointing at the bowl.

"For the house adder," Margo answered with a broad smile, "it's good luck to have a house adder."

"Have you seen any house adders around yet?"

"Not yet, but there must be some around. I have seen two garter snakes already today."

"And why is a house adder good luck?" the husband asked patronizingly. "Because it eats mice?"

"I don't know why," Margo answered with a shrug, "but people who have a house adder under their house always prosper." Margo did not know that her pagan forebears had propitiated the house adder in the belief that it embodied the soul of one of their ancestors.

Gabriel was less interested in house adders than in rattle snakes, because Margo insisted on dismounting whenever she saw an especially beautiful flower.

"You really shouldn't walk through the brush," Gabriel warned, "you might be killed by a snake."

"None of the Salzburgers have been killed yet. Several have been bitten, but none have died."

"What did they do about it?" Gabriel asked.

"While I was at Ebenezer a little girl was bitten on her leg. They put a tourniquet around the leg and sucked the poison out as the Indians do. The leg swelled dreadfully, but she lived. When Ruprecht Steiner was bitten a bit later, someone suggested a better way that was used in Purysburg. They buried Steiner naked up to his neck in the ground so the earth would draw out the poison. He lived, too. And when Paul Müllers' wife was bitten, her husband put the lung and liver of the snake, as well as its backside, on the wound."

"I don't put any more faith in those cures than in snake root," Gabriel vowed. "Perhaps prevention is better than cure."

Two weeks later Gabriel gave Margo a present made by a squaw named Azuki, a pair of deerskin gaiters that reached from shoe to knee and thus protected her from snakebite. After that he was less worried when she picked wild flowers.

"Don't forget," he reminded her, "if you hear a rattle, freeze until you see the snake. Don't try to run away until you see it."

Margo had heard the name Azuki several times and had heard the squaw was a half-breed, and she learned that half-breeds could be very beautiful. Mary Musgrove must have been a beauty when young. Although Gabriel's men always guarded their speech in Margo's presence, she gathered from their conversation that all the traders had squaws, sometimes one at each station. She began to feel a twinge of jealousy towards Azuki, whose name was frequently mentioned in connection with Gabriel. She even heard he occasionally sent her presents.

～

"Couldn't we buy a readymade house from Kogler and live out by our garden?" Margo asked wishfully.

"Not a chance, *Liebchen*," Gabriel answered, affectionately mussing up her carefully combed dark hair. "Military people can never take root. The day you finish your nest you receive orders to move on." *Liebchen* was Gabriel's only term of endearment. But that didn't matter much because every time he said the name "Margo" it sounded like a term of endearment.

One evening a Highlander brought Margo two large shad, both full of roe. He had a gill net that he stretched partially across the river just above the fort. He didn't set the net every day because he caught more fish than he and the garrison could use. The two-month shad run was about to end, and the good people at Fort Argyle had been eating his shad almost daily, until they shuddered at the sight of it. Unfortunately, there was not enough salt to salt the fish, and the inhabitants lacked a smoke house and the knowledge of how to smoke them. Apparently the hogs at Fort Argyle did not tire of such a regular diet.

The same was true of the shad roe, a delicacy of which even a hog can eventually tire. Being a newcomer, Margo ate roe daily for two weeks, until she could no longer stand it.

"I know how you feel," the donor said, when Margo at last declined his gifts. "When I was a lad in the Highlands, we farm laborers signed new contracts every year. We always refused to eat salmon more than three times a week, and we insisted that we get mutton and veal equally often. We did not realize that salmon was a delicacy that few people in England could afford."

~

"Can you swim?" Gabriel asked Margo as soon as the Ogeechee warmed up.

"Not hardly," Margo answered. "There was no swimming hole within ten miles of our village. There wasn't a boy or girl there who ever tried."

"Then it's high time for you to learn," Gabriel insisted, simulating some swimming strokes. "In Georgia you've got to know how to swim. A Salzburger named Arnsdorf fell out of his boat when returning drunk from Purysburg; and our Savannah friend Weissenbacher, of whom even Boltzius approved, drowned when he tried to capture a deer swimming across the Savannah river."

"Well, I don't plan to get drunk in Purysburg, nor do I hope to capture a deer from a canoe."

"But several people in the colony could have avoided capture by Indians if they had known how to swim. It's really necessary."

Margo did not fight the issue. She fabricated a swimming costume from one of Gabriel's old armless vests and cut a pair of his breeches off at the knees. The result was more modest than attractive, and quite a drag in the water. At Ebenezer Margo had bought a housewife, as the British soldiers called the little kit holding scissors, thimble, needles, and thread of various colors and thickness. She also bought some Spanish needles. Boltzius had received a thousand of them from some German benefactor. They came as a charity, and therefore customs-free, but it was obvious that they were sent to be sold.

Gabriel had watched and imitated the older boys playing in the Isar River back in Bavaria and had developed a powerful side stroke. This way of swimming was especially suited to pulling a boat or swimming a horse across a river.

Before instructing Margo, he made her take a deep breath and then exhale slowly with her face under water in a washtub.

"See, you don't have to hold your nose when you go under water. As long as you keep blowing air out of your nose, no water can go up it. Now open your eyes under water and tell me how many fingers I'm holding out." Gabriel suspected that fear of water was partly due to fear of the dark.

Cleaning and inflating two goat stomachs, Gabriel made a pair of water wings that held Margo's head above water while she practiced a frog kick combined with a breast stroke. As her speed gradually increased, Gabriel began decreasing the amount of air in the water wings each time they swam. In a few weeks Margo could swim easily with her almost deflated water wings.

"You don't really need the water wings any more," Gabriel promised her, looking her straight in the eyes with his face somewhat askance, as usual. "See, there is really no air in them."

"Well, perhaps," Margo agreed, throwing the water wings to Gabriel.

"Since we've not yet seen anyone spying on us after so many days, perhaps you could hang your absurd bathing costume next to mine on that cypress knee." After that, Margo glided through the water like a true mermaid.

One warm afternoon while swimming along leisurely, Margo was suddenly confronted by an alligator, one much larger than herself. Turning quickly, she fled so fast that she swam right up on the shore. Her only consolation was Gabriel's assurance that "the alligator was more afraid of you than you were of him, and he turned and swam away even faster than you did." After that, Margo kept closer to Gabriel.

On another occasion while swimming together, they saw Jones' scout boat coming up the river with many passengers. The two naked swimmers hid themselves in the tall reeds, while the boat passed by them.

"Those were Moravians," Gabriel said. "Those pious souls would have been shocked at seeing us."

～

Among the civilians at Fort Argyle was Maria Barbara Roth, whose husband had been evicted from Ebenezer for stirring up discord and disobeying the pastors.

"While I was in Ebenezer," Margo told Gabriel, "I heard that Maria Barbara had disgusted the Salzburgers already on the voyage over by bringing a great quantity of brandy and selling it to her shipmates at un-Christian markups. At Fort Argyle she's again selling at high prices to less provident neighbors."

Margo tried not to be judgmental about Maria Barbara's greed. It was convenient having her little store at hand, even if the markups were a bit un-Christian, to use Boltzius' favorite expression.

～

As the season advanced, Milledge made Gabriel feel right at home and defined the purpose and workings of the little fort.

"Whereas I am the commanding officer here," he informed the newcomer, "you and your Rangers are under the direct command of Captain Mcpherson, a Highlander, whom you may find hard to understand."

"I'm sure we'll get along famously," said Gabriel. "There were several Scots in my troop in Bavaria, and several Irishmen, too."

The Highlander, a rugged redhead, was favorably impressed when Gabriel made his horse step forward, backwards, or sideways and pivot in place.

"What do you call that kind of training?" McPherson asked.

"*Dressage*," Gabriel answered. "I try to follow the practice of the

Spanish Riding School in Vienna, but of course I don't have such good horses to work with."

"It's certainly better than anything I've seen yet in Georgia," the tall cavalryman said, congratulating Gabriel with an approving slap on the shoulder.

"That's partly because the men own their mounts and are proud of them. They are willing to put up with a lot of training."

It was hard for Gabriel to justify such strenuous training except to make the horses respond immediately to their riders' every command.

"I see you don't use a curb bit," McPherson noted with surprise.

"Not necessary. The snaffle's enough and I hardly use it."

This was evident on patrols when Gabriel galloped through the thick woods, jumping over logs and holding his head close to his horse's neck when racing under low branches. While steering his horse, he did not use his bridle, he guided his mount just by shifting the weight of his body. Also, he wore no spurs. He couldn't imagine inflicting such pain or scarring his beautiful steed.

"Now watch this," Gabriel said, drawing his two-foot-long horse pistol from its holster and firing it over Pegasus' head. The horse did not flinch, while all the nearby horses did.

"A calm mount!" McPherson exclaimed.

While the spectators admired the dancing and prancing from left and to right, they saw no sense in it. They had never heard of the cavalry tactic of the *caracole*, which was soon to save Gabriel's life.

"Why do you call your horse Pegasus?" McPherson asked.

"Because that was the name of the best horse in the Riding School while I was there."

"What does it mean?" the Highlander queried.

"No idea," Gabriel admitted.

All agreed the likes of Pegasus were to be found only around Charleston on plantations such as those of the Bulls, Draytons, and Fenwicks. Some people believed Pegasus to be the very horse on which Sir John Fenwick's daughter had eloped with his newly imported English groom. The lovers fled on the morning of her impending marriage to a Drayton heir, but her father's men caught up with them at the Stono Ferry. When a noose was placed around the groom's neck and tied to an overhanging bough, one of the party remonstrated,

"You can't hang a man for stealing a bride!"

"No, but you can hang him for stealing a horse," the outraged father answered, putting a whip in his daughter's hand and forcing her to whip the horse.

5

Ebenezer and Back to Argyle

After some weeks at Fort Argyle, when Gabriel was sent on a three-week mission, Margo decided to spend the time at the Ebenezer orphanage earning some spending money by reeling silk for Mrs. Boltzius, who now managed all the silk production at Ebenezer. Margo liked her employer, a woman only a few years older than herself and equally illiterate.

Barbara Maurer, Margo's sister in sin, briefed her on the Boltzius family.

"Boltzius' young assistant, Israel Gronau, married Catherina Kroeher, a Salzburger girl of eighteen. The marriage was so successful that Boltzius, at thirty-four, married her sister Gertraut, aged seventeen. The widow Kroehr has done well. She's the mother-in-law of the two most eminent men at Ebenezer."

Margo admired the two women, who had become such capable housewives and business women. She did not know she would someday take on just as many responsibilities.

Because Margo lived in the orphanage, which also served as sick bay, she helped with the patients. The most miserable of these during her stay in Ebenezer was Simon Reuter, injured when he treed a bear and shot it. As Boltzius understood it, the bear "had fallen like an ox" and injured Reuter's foot.

"That's what he heard from his Salzburgers," Barbara said, "but he didn't know that in their dialect the word *Fuss* includes the entire leg. Reuter's thigh bone was dislocated."

Margo accompanied the patient to Purysburg, where a French doctor had a device, as painful as any medieval torture rack, on which he could stretch the leg and force it back into the hip socket.

When Margo received her wages for her spinning, her first impulse was to go to Johann Ludwig Meyer's shop and buy a newly imported bonnet. But she could not squander her money. I'll compromise by buying a blue ribbon to decorate my present bonnet. Swiss frugality had won out again against vanity, and the penny saved was a penny earned, one soon hidden in a cubbyhole.

～

During Margo's visit in Ebenezer a German woman named Helena Keller came there to ask Pastor Boltzius to marry her to her elderly black companion. They had been living together for some thirty years and thought it time to be joined in holy wedlock. Boltzius did not wish to marry them and gave legal excuses, but he must have had another reason, too. In Charleston he had seen many mulattos, and he considered miscegenation no better than bestiality.

"How did you come to this country?" Margo asked the woman.

"I was part of the great Palatine immigration of 1710. We had a rough trip and were wrecked on Block Island before reaching New York. The ship was shattered and I was thrown into the sea, unable to swim. Mingo swam out and saved me."

"Is that Mingo?" Margo asked, pointing to the old man.

"Yes," the middle-aged woman answered, "he was a sailor from the Cape Verde Islands, where American whaling vessels used to put in to recruit crewmen. When he took me to his shack and cared for me, I wouldn't let him go, so he missed his ship. He tried to convince me we had no future together. I should go to Pennsylvania where I would quickly find work with the other Dutch and find a husband as soon as I was old enough because there was a great shortage of women."

"And why didn't you take his advice?"

"I guess I was in love with him. He was as handsome as King Balthasar in the nativity plays, and I was grateful."

"Have you lived together ever since?"

"We began living together only after I reached the age of consent. Mingo was very exact in such matters. He became a lobsterman on Cape Cod, a comedown after being a whaler and skillful harpooner. We did rather well, but we never had any children. In the winter he carved oars, walking sticks, spoons, and many other things from wood."

"Is that an example of his work?," Margo asked, pointing to the old man's walking stick. It was an elaborate work of art, apparently of mahogany. There were several stylized heads at the top, and a snake was coiled around the rest of it. Margo had never seen such an excellent piece of wood carving.

"And why are you in Georgia?" Margo asked.

"Mingo's hands swelled up, and I hoped the warm weather in the South would help him. We started south about five years ago, stopping along the way to work as field hands or in any other way. I can still put in a good day's work, but Mingo's hands are so swollen he can just do work fit for children, such as minding cattle or chasing birds from the fields."

Margo was impressed by the woman's self-sacrifice and by the joy with which she made it. She had thought such love was found only in books, in books she could not read. When she offered the woman the few shillings she had with her, the woman declined the offer.

"The Lord has let us support ourselves thus far. We can wait for charity." The woman was right. A Salzburger hired her to hoe and hired her old companion to keep hawks and raccoons from the hen yard.

Boltzius' refusal to marry the mixed couple may have been due in part to his ill humor. He had just learned that a Salzburger woman had let her Palatine servant exorcise her cow. The words of his incantation were:

Little worm, go out of the marrow into the bone bone, Out of the bone into the flesh, out of the flesh
Into the blood, out of the blood into the skin.

"I didn't recite a charm," the servant insisted to Boltzius, "I recited a prayer. In fact I repeated the Lord's Prayer both before it and after it and said it in the name of the Father, Son, and Holy Ghost." The pastor was not fooled. He recognized it as a charm from pagan times and knew that the enchanter was playing God and thus competing with the clergy.

The exorciser did not know the last verse of the ancient charm, which had been, "Out of the skin and into this arrow." The medicine man then shot the arrow deep into the forest.

Margo was surprised at Boltzius' reaction. "My father," she later confessed to Gabriel, "always called on a wise old neighbor woman to exorcise his cattle when they were sick, and her charms usually succeeded in driving out the greedy worm and saving the beast."

～

Margo received her earnings in scrip, little pieces of paper marked two pence, three pence, six pence, and a shilling, each of them signed personally by Pastor Boltzius. Otherwise there was no small currency in and around Ebenezer, because all coins flowed at once to the merchants in Savannah. Boltzius had received two large kegs of pennies, but these had soon fallen out of circulation. Because small coins were in short supply, most petty trade had to be conducted by barter, which was time-consuming and unpredictable. Therefore everyone was glad to accept the little paper notes. As the notes became too worn through use, Boltzius replaced them with new ones.

～

When Margo finished her silk reeling and Gabriel came to escort her home, they carried a message from Boltzius to a Salzburger named Lemmenhofer, whose plantation lay about three miles from Ebenezer. Margo was appalled at the sallow faces, bloated bellies, and spindle legs of three of the four Lemmenhofer children.

Waiting to be out of hearing distance, Margo asked, "What is the matter with those children?"

"They are clay-eaters, *Liebchen*," Gabriel answered, reaching over to caress her neck.

"What's that?"

"The children eat clay, dirt, sand, ashes, and things like that."

"Don't their parents tell them not to?"

"Of course they do, but the children do it anyway, despite very severe whippings when they are caught. Boltzius even threatens them with divine punishment for this sin."

"Why is it a sin?" Margo asked.

"Because it's suicide, if you believe in the fifth commandment."

"Couldn't the clay-eating be the result rather than the cause of the illness? There must some reason for the children's irresistible craving to eat dirt, especially when they know that they are going to be so severely punished in both this world and the next."

"I think you have something there," Gabriel conceded, "but it would be hard to prove. I am glad to see that you are willing to reject common knowledge. When I first knew you, I didn't believe you could think for yourself. You used to believe anything you were supposed to believe. You even let Boltzius keep you from staying with Stout."

"There was nothing else I could do."

"Sure there was. You and Stout could have run off to Orangeburg, where the pastor is not so demanding. Milledge and the Schneider women would have let you go. But thank God you didn't," he added, giving her an affectionate slap on the backside, "or I wouldn't have you now."

Margo was dying to ask Gabriel about Azuki, but she was too proud to reveal her suspicions, which were surely and certainly unjustified, she hoped. Instead, she suffered in silence and pretended that the squaw did not exist.

Soon after Gabriel left on one of his longer missions a new Ranger was added to the troop. He was very handsome and well aware of it, and quite sure that three weeks was long enough for him to have his way with the lovely straw-widow. Margo resented his advances. She even refused to join the occasional dances so as to avoid having to dance with him or to create a scene by refusing. When he persisted, Margo went to Gabriel's corporal Lightner with a request.

"Please tell Ellsworth that Gabriel is the best shot in the regiment and very, very jealous." The unwanted attentions quickly stopped.

Lightner and his friend Rowner were Gabriel's favorite corporals. The English sergeant who recruited them had preserved the exact pronunciation of the original names Leitner and Rauner. They were a discrepant couple. Rowner was short and heavy set, and his bullet-shaped head seemed to rest directly on his broad shoulders. If he'd had a neck, he would have been of average height. His high tenor voice came as a surprise from such a solid body, and he usually stuttered. Before speaking, he always scratched behind his right ear.

Lightner was a full head taller than his companion, but thin and wiry. Before speaking, no matter how trivial the subject, he always cleared his throat as if he were about to make an important pronouncement. His basso profundo voice came unexpectedly in view of his slender and almost delicate build. Lightner had a peculiar mannerism, too. He constantly put his right hand to his right temple to push his thinning hair over his hairless pate. As a result, he constantly appeared to be returning an ungiven salute.

The two men reminded Margo of Boltzius and Gronau. Because of his authoritative air and imposing presence, Boltzius loomed large when standing alone, but he shrank to human proportions when his adoring assistant, Israel Gronau, stood next to him a head taller. The same was true of John Wesley, who looked tall when alone in his clerical gown but was far below average in height.

~

Thomas Bichler, Ebenezer's corpulent constable, came one day to Fort Argyle to ask Gabriel for help. He, too, had a clay-eating daughter, but that was not the reason for this visit.

"I want you to help me catch the Spaniard."

"Who's he?" Gabriel asked.

"An unsavory character, a dark-skinned fellow with shoulder length black hair. He's a highwayman who makes the local trails unsafe for the Salzburgers, most of whom go unarmed. He isn't violent. In fact no one has yet been killed, but perhaps only because no one has resisted him."

"What does he take?"

"He demands tribute, Sergeant. Sometimes a horse or a cow, but usually just a saddle or powder horn or whatever else he needs at the moment. Many think he's a deserter from Saint Augustine. He may have been a convicted criminal deported to America for compulsory labor, but his skilful riding suggests he was once in military service."

Bichler had tried many times to catch the brigand, who was always long since gone by the time the eager lawman reached the scene of the crime.

"I guess I'm just not as good a horseman as the Spaniard is. Besides that, he has a much better horse."

Bichler was right, his horse was bred for pulling wagons, not for catching outlaws. Gabriel asked the portly constable to tell him all he knew about the robber, and then he made a sketch of the area and trails surrounding Ebenezer. Next he marked the location and date of the most recent robberies in hopes of discovering a pattern. With some logic and much speculation, he and Bichler surmised where and when the next crime might occur.

"It's a far-out chance, but better than nothing," Gabriel said, "since we have no other leads."

At dawn two days later, Bichler and Gabriel were both riding on the trail leading from Fort Argyle to Fort Mount Pleasant, a little fortress and ferry landing on the Savannah River about twenty-five miles above Ebenezer and across from Oglethorpe's slave-operated barony near Palachacola. Bichler was riding southward from Mt. Pleasant while Gabriel was riding northward from Fort Argyle. By high noon they were still about six miles apart. Some three miles along the way, Bichler saw a horseman approaching him from the south. He held his ground.

Seeing the constable armed, the highwayman turned and galloped south, for he preferred unarmed victims. Bichler followed at a safe distance and blew his hunting horn after another mile, estimating that Gabriel was now in hearing distance.

Recognizing the horn's signal, Gabriel knew the brigand was approaching. I can easily conceal myself in the undergrowth and shoot the poor bastard, Gabriel thought, but that would be too easy, and very unsporting. I'd rather meet him face to face. Whistling to Kumpan to stay, Gabriel moved to a spot where the trail entered an open savanna.

Seeing Gabriel blocking the way, the Spaniard stopped his horse, shouldered his flintlock and aimed.

"Now's the time," Gabriel said to Pegasus, patting him on the withers and signaling with his heel. Pegasus performed his best *caracole*, the intricate dance step to right and to left and too irregular to predict. The Spaniard tried to aim, but every time he was about to squeeze his trigger, he saw that his target was no longer in his sights.

Gabriel was approaching closer and closer, dancing from left to right and back again. At about ten yards he drew his saber from its scabbard, charged forward, and quickly split the highwayman's head almost in two. His victim fell with a thump, never having fired his piece. Bichler arrived a few minutes later and the two men put the bloody corpse on his horse and took him and his musket to Ebenezer, to the great joy of all the inhabitants. With much pleasure the Salzburgers buried their tormenter naked in the *Schindanger*, the field where they buried carrion, far from holy ground.

"I'll just take the silver bridle and the ornate saddle," Gabriel suggested, "and you can take the musket and the horse, which is so much faster than your own."

"Many thanks. That's most generous."

"And Kumpan will get the food the highwayman was carrying. I guess Pegasus will just have to wait for his reward, unless some grateful Salzburger happens to have a load of hay or oats."

❧

Another suspicious person was lurking around in Georgia at that time. He told the British authorities his name was Joseph Anthony Mazzique and that he was a surgeon from Old Castile. Milledge questioned the name:

"It's not Spanish but French, and it's the name of one of the most prominent Huguenot families in Carolina."

"He told Boltzius his name was Masig and he was from Cologne," Margo interposed, "but that seems unlikely since he is so swarthy."

Because Mazzique was not practicing surgery and had no visible means of support, he was generally thought to be a spy for the Spaniards at Saint Augustine. Besides, it looked strange for a surgeon to carry two pistols in his belt. Gabriel was ordered to keep an eye on him, but their trails had not yet crossed.

❧

Fort Argyle was located on the post road Oglethorpe had blazed to Frederica with the help of the Creek Indians. Its purpose was to prevent the Florida Indians, or Spanish Indians as they were usually called, from raiding Georgia and South Carolina. Spain and England were now engaged in the War of Jenkins' Ear.

"Why is it called the War of Jenkins' Ear?" Margo asked Captain Milledge.

"Because a Spanish customs official cut off the ear of an English smuggler named Jenkins," the casually dressed officer answered, simulating the amputation of an ear. "Jenkins pickled his ear in a jar and took it to Parliament and showed it around until the members finally declared war to vindicate England's honor.

"The real cause of the war," the youthful captain continued, "was that His Most Catholic Majesty resents Oglethorpe's encroachment on lands claimed by Spain. The Spaniards claim all the lands as far north as Port Royal in South Carolina, while Oglethorpe lays claim to all the lands between the Savannah and the Altamaha Rivers."

"But Frederica is south of the Altamaha," Margo protested.

"Oglethorpe fixed that."

"How?" Margo asked.

"He altered a map to show an imaginary estuary of the Altamaha running southeast in a straight line all the way into the Saint John's River in Spanish territory. Thus he made Saint Simons Island the property of the English. This forgery was printed as authentic."

"I don't think a gentleman like Oglethorpe would do something like that," Margo declared, coming to the defense of her hero.

~

One day at high noon Gabriel received orders to accompany Joseph Watson, an official in Savannah, on his way to a talk with the Upper Creeks at their main town of Cuweta. Gabriel was gone a long time, and Margo missed him greatly. When he finally reappeared with a dispatch for Captain Milledge, everyone crowded around to hear the latest news and hardly let him greet Margo. Suddenly, Gabriel suffered a seizure.

"Don't be alarmed," Margo urged the worried crowd. "He often has such attacks. He just has to rest for a half an hour."

With help from two of the guests, she led her ailing husband to their quarters next door. Once across their threshold, Margo slammed the door and lifted the heavy bolt into its slots. In a half hour they returned to the assembled well-wishers and relieved them of their anxiety about Gabriel's health.

～

Among Gabriel's duties at Fort Argyle was capturing runaway slaves on their way from South Carolina to Florida, where the Spanish governor had promised them sanctuary. Gabriel found this service as odious as helping the archbishop expel the Salzburger peasants while he was serving in the Imperial cavalry. Once, when Gabriel was returning to Fort Argyle with a black prisoner, Margo came out to meet him on the trail. She at once felt pity for the poor, tightly bound captive, who appeared half-starved and exhausted.

"Look how badly his back is scarred," Margo gasped.

"Probably from previous whippings for trying to escape," Gabriel suggested. "He must be a recently imported African and not yet broken in. He can't speak much English."

Margo could not communicate with the prisoner, but she did give him the food she had brought for her husband. She finally prevailed on Gabriel to free his captive even though it would cost him his share of the bounty and he would have to reward his two Indian guides from his own pocket. Free of his bonds, the miserable creature disappeared into the forest carrying Margo's loaf of bread and a roasted passenger pigeon.

"You wouldn't have done that two years ago," Gabriel said, caressing Margo's hand.

"Why not?"

"The slaves on the plantations around Stono Ferry just outside of Charleston revolted and killed all the whites they could find, women and children included."

"What happened then?"

"The rebellion spread rapidly at first but gradually petered out because of poor leadership and too much pilfered rum. The local white militia under William Bull easily suppressed the revolt and killed all the ringleaders. Just the ringleaders, of course, because slaves are too valuable to kill just for revenge."

Gabriel and his hound also captured white runaways. The deserters from Frederica he escorted back to their units, where they were duly whipped. He interrogated the indentured servants from Savannah and listened to their complaints.

"Why did you run away?" was his standard question.

"Because my master beat me and starved me," was a typical answer.

"Do you have any scars?" If these were visible, and if the bearer was young and able-bodied, Gabriel would ask, "Would you rather be returned to your master or sign up in the military at Frederica under an assumed name?" Most chose the second alternative, thereby rendering it all the more difficult for the Trustees to make an accurate count of Georgia's inhabitants.

Gabriel often carried dispatches to and from Fort Mount Venture, a little stockade on the Altamaha in the "debatable land". The fort was insignificant, being garrisoned by only Lt. William Francis and four enlisted men. Learning that his sweetheart in Savannah, an indentured Palatine girl, was pregnant, the lieutenant returned to that city and made an honest woman of her, to the amusement of the gossipy Colonel Stephens. Within three months the lieutenant's wife bore him a son.

While sharpening his saber one morning, Gabriel spoke to Lieutenant Francis in his broken English, and the lieutenant answered in perfect German.

"Where did you learn German?" the astonished trooper asked.

"At my mother's knee," the lieutenant answered. "I was born in Heilbronn, but I served in a British regiment for five years before being sent here to Georgia. I used to be Wilhelm Franz."

On his fourth trip to Fort Mount Venture, Gabriel found only the mutilated bodies of the lieutenant's wife and child. The fort had been captured by Indians and the four-man garrison had been taken prisoner. Kumpan tracked the war party to the Satilla River but lost the trail at a point where they must have concealed their dugouts during the raid.

Later on, Gabriel learned from Solomon Schad, one of the two survivors, that the lieutenant had been in Savannah during the attack and that, when the Indians set fire to the fort, the garrison had surrendered under promise of safe-conduct to Saint Augustine.

On their way to Florida the Indians reconsidered, held a powwow, and killed and scalped two of their four prisoners. A little later, they stopped, argued a bit more, and then sent back two of their party to tomahawk the commander's wife and child. They must have remembered another old score to settle, some ancient point of honor.

While the war party was approaching Saint Augustine, one of the two surviving captives escaped into a swamp and eventually made his way to Savannah. The other, Solomon Schad, was sold to the Spaniards in Saint Augustine, who exchanged him for a Spanish prisoner of war in Savannah. Later Schad became a prosperous taverner in Savannah.

❧

"Why are the Indians so cruel?" Margo asked when Gabriel returned home and told his story.

"I suppose they know not what they do, like Christ's crucifiers. We Europeans have had the gospel for more than a thousand years, yet we still kill people. They have not yet heard the Sermon on the Mount."

"But the Indians kill women and children!"

"Very prudent. If you kill all the squaws and papooses, there will be fewer braves to kill later on."

After the bloody massacre at Fort Mount Pleasant, Gabriel became more serious and fearful for Margo's life, since Fort Argyle was not much better defended than Lieutenant Francis' little stockade. For greater security, he mounted even more patrols.

Margo saw less and less of her husband, and her sleep was often disturbed by gnawing night hunger caused by his absence. Does he miss me as much as I miss him? she wondered. How does such a virile man contain himself on such long journeys? Or does he? I'm curious about his relationship with Azuki, but I refuse to be jealous. Margo had seen how severe the Indians could be to adulteresses, and even to unfaithful widows. But she also knew how promiscuous Indian girls could be. A child by an Indian trader was a blessing rather than a curse, especially if it had blue eyes or fair hair. She guessed that was why so many of the chiefs had European features and coloring.

71

Margo listened attentively to the gossipy Rangers, but they minded their speech in her presence. She did, however, hear the name Azuki mentioned from time to time. She learned that Gabriel had ordered one of his men to accompany the squaw from Palachocola to a spot near Mary Musgrove's cattle pen, where he built a hut for her. Why would he keep her so far away? Margo's pride kept her from investigating.

∼

To pass her time by day and to escape her jealousy, Margo took service with Mrs. Milledge, the commandant's wife. Thus she could learn English ways of housekeeping and see the children more often. She also strove to learn the English language, for which she had an unusual aptitude but little opportunity to hear it among the polyglot troopers. She quickly learned all the words used by the Milledge children.

Margo often saw Mrs. Milledge engrossed in a book. How she envied her for being able to read! If only I could have gone to school! Margo particularly resented the competition of *Tom Jones*, which occupied her mistress in her few leisure hours and left little time for idle chatter. Therefore, for sociability, she spent most evenings with Gabriel and his troopers sharing their small talk, which was corrupted by Gaelic, French, and German of a half dozen dialects.

Kumpan profited from these social evenings around the iron stove in the squad room. Margo picked ticks off Kumpan, who was badly plagued by them. At first she just pulled the ticks off, to Kumpan's great discomfort, and left the tick's pincers in his skin, where they later festered.

"That's not the way to do it, Ma'am," the lanky corporal Lightner told her in his basso profundo voice, brushing the hair from the side of his head to cover his balding pate. "Hold a burning ember over the tick like this, and it'll loosen its hold to escape the heat."

Margo took the stick, with one end still burning, and made the tick pull out its pincers. Then she threw her victim on the red hot cast iron stove, where it popped and sizzled. She was joined in this sport by other dog owners, and the stove popped and sizzled steadily.

∼

In time Gabriel commanded a detachment of twenty horsemen,

whom he exercised daily in the art of war, particularly in the *caracole* that had recently saved his life. When drilling at the fort, he wore the uniform in which he had left the count's service and which, along with his boots, kepi, compass, and field glass, he had brought in his second duffle bag. His tight red jacket emphasized his broad shoulders and slender waist; and Margo was rightly proud of her handsome husband with his plumed kepi and military moustache. She also admired his flaxen hair, which he wore cut short.

"Why do you cut your hair so short?" she asked.

"Gustavus Adolphus wore his hair that way, and we do it in his honor." That meant nothing to Margo.

On his patrols, Gabriel dressed inconspicuously like his men, there being no standard uniform. His men wore whatever they could find, provided it blended with the forest, for they usually fought dismounted. Since the forests in southern Georgia are green all year, they preferred green clothing, often with brown patches sewed on them. The men served most often as mounted infantry. They used their horses to reach the battlefield, but they fought on foot. The cavalry tactics Gabriel taught them were spectacular, but they were of little use in the jungle.

Gabriel told Margo little about his adventures, fearing they might upset her. She kept abreast, however, by questioning his men in his absence. They proudly related all his foolhardy actions, and they praised him as the greatest of all leaders.

"The sergeant sure don't know what fear is, Ma'am," Rowner assured Margo, scratching behind his left ear. "He don't think of no danger."

Margo sighed, "I wish he did think of danger and would fear it sometimes. I would rather have a live husband than a dead hero."

"I'll be sure to tell the old man that."

"What old man?"

"Sergeant Bach."

"Gabriel is not old!"

"He's the senior non-com around here, so he's the old man. Even Corporal Jefferson calls him the 'old man', and he's sixty-two."

6

Panzer

For her safety, Gabriel taught Margo to ride, not sidesaddle like the Carolina gentlewomen, but astride like his Rangers. For this purpose she made herself a pair of pantaloons so full that, when she was standing, they looked like a full skirt. Her little mare, Betsy, was a marsh tackey, a breed of wild horses found on the coastal islands. They were descended from survivors of shipwrecks or from horses thrown overboard to lighten ships in a storm. It did not take Gabriel long to teach Margo how to post when her little mare trotted, and it took even less time for her to keep her seat when Betsy galloped or jumped. Gabriel also taught Margo to shoot a pistol, even at a full gallop.

One morning, while they were riding together toward Ebenezer, the young equestrians heard a dog yelping ferociously. Approaching the commotion, they found a little cur barking up a tree.

"Look up there!" Gabriel said, pointing to the lowest bough.

"I don't see anything."

"Look again." Margo looked up into the tree and saw a tyger crouched on one of the limbs.

"Here, take this pistol and shoot."

Gabriel handed Margo his double-barreled horse pistol. She held it with both hands, aimed carefully at the beast's heart, and fired the right barrel, which was rifled and therefore more accurate than any smoothbore musket three times its length. The recoil almost knocked Margo off her mare, which jumped in alarm, while Pegasus stood by calmly. The big cat fell with a thud, writhed on the ground a moment, gave birth to two spotted cubs, and died.

"This animal," Margo informed Gabriel, "is not nearly as large as the tyger shot by John Stout, yet it is still much taller and longer than any hound I have ever seen, even taller and longer than Kumpan." Suddenly she felt remorse for killing an animal in the family way.

Gabriel put the two cubs into Margo's saddle bag and was just lifting the dead beast up onto Pegasus when a Salzburger named Riedelsperger came running up with a musket.

"I see you've killed my tyger," he said disappointedly. "I was chopping wood when my dog treed it, so I ran back home to get my gun. But now I see you got here first."

"She's all yours," Gabriel volunteered. "Rather, by rights she belongs to your little dog."

Gabriel and Riedelsberger heaved the big cat up onto Pegasus and carried it to Ebenezer so Riedelsperger could show it off. By chance, an English naturalist was stopping there on one of his scientific expeditions.

"That's neither a tiger nor a lion," he declared, "but a panther, usually called a puma, cougar, or mountain lion."

"That must be the reason the people from Carolina and Virginia call it a painter," Riedelsperger suggested.

Finding a Salzburger woman who owned a nursing bitch, Gabriel paid her to let his cubs suckle with her puppies. The puppies were already several weeks old and therefore about the same size as the newborn cubs. A few weeks later, however, the woman protested, "The cubs are too big and competitive for their litter mates. I know a woman whose nanny goat will nurse the cubs, provided it's held down while doing so."

Eventually, when the cubs were weaned, Gabriel employed the Purysburg butcher, Johann Altherr, to take over their nourishment with scrap meat. Gabriel had noted that the balls regurgitated by falcons and hawks and the droppings left by wild cats and panthers consist mostly of fur, feathers, bones, and teeth.

"When you feed the cats," he ordered the barrel-chested butcher, "give them mostly chicken necks. If you give them meat or entrails, be sure they are covered with feathers." Altherr thought him mad. In Savannah, Altherr was known as the "Dutch butcher", even though he was a Swiss.

When the male cub died, for reasons unknown, Gabriel took the surviving female with him on his travels, first in a saddle bag and later on a leather pad on the horse's croup.

～

"I'm not happy with this addition to the family," Margo confessed, "I'm no Patient Griselda."

Nevertheless, still a docile wife, she put up with it and helped with the feeding, giving Panzer, as the cub was now called, an occasional pan of milk until she no longer accepted it. Not yet able to pronounce English *th*, Margo and Gabriel pronounced the word "panther" as "panzer," and that is the way their friends heard the name.

Poor Kumpan, now of a sedate age, quickly tired of playing with the frolicsome young cat, which would snarl and bare its fangs at Kumpan until he did likewise, although the hound would have preferred to sleep. When Kumpan refused to snarl any more, Panzer would cuddle up and sleep with him.

Patting Kumpan on his head, Gabriel said, "I see that Panzer is also getting on well with Pegasus, who seems to enjoy having company in his stall. Panzer won't deign to eat a rat, but her very presence is keeping all the rats away." As Panzer matured, she lost her spots and took on the sorrel color of her late mother.

On the road, Gabriel experienced little difficulty in feeding his new riding companion. If he shot a deer, bear, or wild pig, he disemboweled it on the spot and gave her and Kumpan the entrails, which they greatly preferred to steaks. If he failed to shoot any large game, he would use the unrifled barrel loaded with scatter shot to bring down a rabbit, wood duck, passenger pigeon, or fox squirrel. He never killed a grey or cat squirrel. It's meat would not have justified the powder or shot.

When Panzer reached full size, Margo said, "Panzer is larger than any hound I've ever seen, including Kumpan, yet she still behaves like all the house cats I've ever known. She loves to cuddle up and feign great affection, which isn't very convincing, just to be scratched under her chin. It's lucky she always remembers to keep her claws sheathed."

Once Panzer was full grown, she spent much of her time ranging on the ground along with Kumpan, circling Pegasus to flush game and chase it into Gabriel's range. Then, when tired, she would jump, ever so lightly, back onto her pad on Pegasus' croup and ride as proudly as any mahara-jah on his howdah. When Margo was with Gabriel at Fort Argyle, she took over the task of feeding the beast.

"I sure can't teach Panzer anything," she complained. "You can teach Kumpan anything you want, but Panzer just won't learn.

"It's much easier to teach Pegasus," Gabriel agreed.

"Couldn't we teach her to retrieve?"

"Not a chance, *Liebchen*, Gabriel contended. If I throw out a stick, she ignores it. If I throw out a piece of meat, she eats it."

"You know what I like most about Panzer?"

"What?"

"Her fur. It's as tawny as your mustache. Of course she's not as blond as your sun-bleached hair."

When mentioning Gabriel's mustache, Margo remembered the old Spanish proverb: "A kiss without a moustache is like eggs without pepper." Was the proverb true? Perhaps it just meant that kissing a beardless boy was unexciting. Gabriel would be kissable with or without a mustache, she assured herself.

∼

One afternoon Gabriel and Margo happened to be riding near Riedelsperger's plantation and decided to stop in to see what he had done with his panther skin. The Salzburger proudly showed them the hide, now well-cured. He had taken out the skull, boiled it, and removed all the meat. Next he put the skull, complete with big painted wooden eyes, back into the skin of the head. This made an attractive floor mat, and the cat's malevolent eyes followed the viewer no matter where he stood.

"Would you like some peach brandy?" Riedelsperger asked, pour-ing a large tumbler full of the aromatic liqueur. "Boltzius doesn't like us to drink rum, which is strong and illegal; but he can't very well keep us from drinking brandy, since our still was given to us by the SPCK."

"What's the SPCK?" Margo asked Riedelsperger.

"The Society for Promoting Christian Knowledge. It's the mission-ary society in London that pays our preachers and schoolmaster."

After a few rounds of brandy, the company became merry; and Riedelsperger, a bit mellow, sang a sentimental Salzburger folksong about green meadows and the sorrow of parting. Gabriel followed with a soldier song, also dealing with the sorrow of leaving loved ones. Margo sang a pastoral song ending in a yodel. Before she finished, two little shoats came running up expectantly.

"What do the pigs want?" she asked.

"You've just called them," Riedelsperger explained. "They are expecting some food."

"Why so?" Margo asked.

"During the last five years," the Salzburger answered, "so many Swiss on the frontier have been calling their pigs by yodeling that the English and Scots farmers have begun calling their pigs in a falsetto voice, too. Now it is called 'hawg-calling' or 'hollering'. If you don't want pigs, you had better not yodel."

On the way home, while Panzer was trotting alongside, Gabriel said, "I feel like Iwain."

"Who was he?" Margo asked.

"The hero of *The Knight with the Lion*, which my grandmother used to tell me. Once upon a time a brave knight rescued a lion from a dreadful dragon. The grateful lion then accompanied him on all his daring adventures. Eventually the lion saved his benefactor from two wicked giants, but it died in doing so."

"I hope you are not counting on Panzer coming to your rescue if you are attacked by two wicked giants. Kumpan might do that, but I'm sure Panzer would only think of herself. I've never had much faith in feline fidelity."

Gabriel could hardly disagree with this judgment. He was pleased to see Margo's growing self-assurance.

~

For their love-making Margo and Gabriel created their own arcane language. Finding standard words either too vulgar or too clinical for their intimacies, they gradually built up a secret language to designate their body parts, actions, and feelings, a language known only to them.

While speaking this private language Margo never thought of Azuki, who loomed large only when she was alone and lonesome.

One evening, after an especially rewarding session in bed, Margo asked, "Does everyone do this?"

"Why, of course."

"Even the peasants?"

"Yes indeed."

"Then have them stop at once! It's too good for them!"

In her own eyes Margo was no longer a peasant, she was the lawful wife of a sergeant. Gabriel had never heard her joke this way, especially about such a serious subject.

While Margo and Gabriel were riding cross-country one fair day, Gabriel shouted,

"Watch out for that gopher hole!" Margo saw the hole in time and turned Betsy away from it.

"I thought a gopher was a little rodent. How could it make such a large hole?"

"Around here the word 'gopher' doesn't mean a rodent. It means a land tortoise that makes holes large enough to break a horse's leg. Fortunately, Pegasus always sees them in time, and I hope Betsy will too. In cold weather the holes are sometimes full of rattlesnakes."

A little bit farther on, Margo saw a sunlit glade covered with white blossoms. This brought her great joy, because she had not seen the sun for weeks. The tops of the immense longleaf pines and cypresses at Fort Argyle formed such a dense canopy that hardly a ray of light could shine through except where Margo had ringed the trees, and she had not seen a sunrise or sunset for many weeks. She trotted Betsy into the sunlit glade until they were suddenly in four feet of water. The flowers, native white water lilies, put out large floating leaves so close together that they looked like a blooming meadow.

"Why didn't you tell me?" Margo scolded.

"You didn't ask me," Gabriel answered. "That's a lily pond. The floating plants get their nourishment by anchoring their roots onto the bottom." At least Margo enjoyed the lilies' delightful fragrance.

A few nights later Captain Milledge invited all his men and their families to a barbecue, the first Margo ever attended and the first time she ever heard the word "barbecue". The two main courses, served on large wooden platters, were venison and roasted turkey, both gifts from Gabriel. There were also catfish, hominy grits, and sweet potatoes, as well as a jug of rum.

After the meal, the neckless Rowner brought out two croaker sacks, as burlap bags were called in Georgia. He untied one and shook it, and out slid a large rattlesnake. Instead of slithering away, the snake coiled and shook its rattles. The trooper then opened the other sack and poured out a long black snake. It, too, did not try to escape, rather it eyed the rattlesnake attentively.

Margo studied the black snake. "What kind of snake is the long thin one?"

"It's a coachwhip," Gabriel answered. "The English naturalist who passed through Ebenezer a couple of weeks ago said it is a kind of boa constrictor. You'll soon see why."

After sizing up its prey, the coachwhip coiled near the rattler, but just out of reach. It then began teasing its victim. When it thrust its head close, the poisonous viper lunged but missed. The second time the coachwhip probed, the rattler struck again. This time the black snake dodged and caught the rattler by its neck, just behind its head. Then, quicker than the spectators could see, it wrapped itself around the heavy serpent several times and slowly squeezed.

"But how is such a skinny snake going to swallow such a thick one with its small head and mouth?" Margo asked Gabriel.

"You'll see."

When the rattler stopped struggling, the coachwhip loosened a joint on each side of its jaw, thus making its mouth twice as large. It then slowly spread its extended mouth over its victim's head.

"Why is the blacksnake eating so slowly?"

"Because the rattler's too dry. Most people think snakes are slimy, but actually they are very dry. The coachwhip has to moisten its prey, I suppose with its tongue, to make it slippery enough to go down. It will be a slow job."

Gabriel was right. It took the constrictor at least twenty minutes to swallow its victim. Somehow its elastic body could stretch far enough to accommodate itself to the much thicker victim. When the greatly distended victor finished its meal, its owner put it back into the sack. Margo found the whole spectacle revolting, yet somehow fascinating. Two years earlier it would have turned her stomach.

~

A week later Gabriel borrowed a dugout, a canoe carved out of a single cypress log.

"This is an Indian canoe," he explained to Margo.

"But how did the Indians chisel out the wood before they got iron tools from the whites?"

"I have heard that they burned away the excess wood, but I don't see how that was possible."

Gabriel also borrowed a long bamboo pole and a half dozen fish hooks from a fellow trooper. Tying the hooks to the tip of a deer tail to make a bob, he fastened the bob directly to the small end of the pole. Margo took her seat amidship in the dugout and Gabriel showed her what to do.

"Grasp the pole with your left hand about three feet from its thick end, like this. While I'm paddling the canoe close along the shore, hold the pole across the dugout with your left hand resting on your crossed knees. Then beat on the thick end of the pole with your fist, like this." This made the hook-studded deer tail at the other end of the pole jump up and down noisily on the water.

Because there was no line, Margo could thrust the jerking bait between fallen logs and between cypress knees, where no one could cast a line. In a short time she hooked a fish and lifted the pole, but then the fish was hanging in the air fifteen feet above her head.

"Don't lift it up," Gabriel ordered. "Let it down again and just pull the pole in hand over hand like a rope." Margo did as ordered and found she had caught a bluegill scarcely larger than the bait.

81

"Why did such a little fish try to eat such a big bait?"

"It didn't try to eat it. It was just trying to chase the bait away from its nest. That's why we use so many hooks. It didn't bite, it was just snagged." Margo felt rather contemptible catching the brave little defender of its nest.

The next catch was a different story. The victim was so heavy Margo could not lift it. Then, remembering Gabriel's orders, she pulled the pole in hand over hand to the boat and lifted aboard a fourteen pound trout, as the local English called largemouth bass.

"Well done," Gabriel congratulated. "That's more than we need, but we can catch more for my troopers." By evening Margo had caught a dozen or more fish, varying in size from her bluegill to her trout.

Margo's next fishing expedition was unplanned. There had been no rain for some weeks, and the Ogeechee had fallen to a record low. As a result, the sloughs on either side of the river had largely dried up, leaving all their many catfish stranded in little puddles. As she and Gabriel were crossing one of the dried up sloughs their horses frightened away a bear, which was catching catfish in one of the shallow puddles. The young couple rode to the spot and found the puddle literally filled with catfish.

"Don't let them sting you," Gabriel warned, as Margo tried to help him put some of them in his sack. "Their fins are poisonous and very painful. I don't know how the bears can eat them." He took as many as he could use and then left the rest for the bear, which had been watching them resentfully at a short distance.

On their way home Margo noted that she always sidled up to Gabriel so close that their stirrups often touched. Sometimes this was because the path was narrow, but it also occurred when the path was amply wide for two to ride abreast. She was not conscious of deliberately closing in on her partner. Did Gabriel exude some sort of animal magnetism on me? she asked herself. Then, reflecting, she rephrased the question. Did Pegasus exude animal magnetism on Betsy?

～

A few evenings later Gabriel had a guest named Wiggins, the first Indian trader Margo ever met. He had just returned from a long inspection tour of all the English trading houses among the Chickasaws and Cherokees, which tribes he greatly preferred to the local Creeks. Margo was full of questions.

"Is it very dangerous living among the Indians?"

"No danger at all from the host tribe," the lean-faced trader assured her, emptying another glass of port. "If a trader's killed, it's by enemies of the host tribe. Of course many of the traders are heavy drinkers and sometimes fight to the finish with one of their hosts, but that's rare, 'cause the chiefs break up the fight to save the trader."

"But why do the Indians protect their traders, especially when they cheat them so shamefully?"

"The Indians can't live without the traders," the red-bearded frontiersman replied. "They depend on them for fire arms and fire water. Without gunpowder from the trader the Indians would be at the mercy of neighboring tribes who have a trader, and without rum the chief could not buy the loyalty of many braves. Also, since the introduction of fire arms, game has become more cautious. It's hard now to get into bow and arrow range of a deer. Because some Indians have guns, all of them must have guns."

"Sounds like a vicious circle," Margo said. Gabriel wondered where she had learned such a fancy terms.

"The Indians' biggest enemy is rum," the long-bearded Indian trader continued. "They can neither hold it nor abstain from it. Most sober Indians are kind and generous, while most drunk ones are mean and dangerous."

"Why do they fight each other all the time? Wouldn't they do better to unite and fight together against the whites?"

"They have no concept of being Indians. There is no word for Indians in their languages. They have words for Creeks, Chickasaws, and Cherokees, but none for Indians; and every tribe welcomes the white man's help in destroying its neighbors. Up there in the Indian country there's a mad man named Prieber who's trying to unite the Indians, but he won't get far."

Margo paid close attention to all this, knowing that Gabriel was often among the Indians.

83

7

From Argyle to Frederica

On her forays with Gabriel, Margo always enjoyed the flowers, of which she often picked enough to make a wreath. Gabriel urged her to ride without a bonnet, he enjoyed seeing her rich hair blowing freely in the wind, especially when she was wearing a colorful wreath. Margo's favorite flower was the yellow jasmine, which emitted a delightful aroma.

"The nice thing about this climate," Margo said, pointing to some honeysuckle blossoms, "is that there is always something in bloom no matteer what the season."

"I don't suppose you've found any edelweis?"

"No, not yet, but I've found a lot of other beauties, such as flowering dogwood, azaleas, irises, magnolias, lotus, and sunbonnets. I think that is what Mrs. Milledge calls them. I enjoy identifying some of them by their aromas. What are your favorite flowers, Gabriel?"

"My favorite flowers are black walnuts, grapes, false dandelions, acorns, roots, chinquapins, cabbage palmettoes, and huckleberries, and other berries that can keep you alive in dire necessity. Their taste and smell don't matter much when you are starving."

On one occasion Gabriel did take an interest in a flower Margo showed him, but only because some bees were gathering nectar from it.

"Stay where you are till I get back," Gabriel ordered. He went to their nearby quarters and returned with a flat shingle, some damp raw sugar, and a small glass jar. Putting the sugar on the shingle, he placed it under the flower and then brought the jar down on it, thereby capturing the flower and the bees in it.

The bees flew around angrily until they noticed the sugar, which they at once began to garner. Gabriel then removed the jar and let the bees return to their hive with their booty. He did not have to wait long for the bees to return with helpers to harvest the sugar on the shingle. As soon as there was a steady stream of bees coming from and going to the hive, he followed them slowly to their hive in a dead oak tree.

"Now that you have found the hive," Margo asked, "how are you going to get the honey?"

"That's your job," Gabriel answered, caressing Margo's forearm. "The blacks who taught the Salzburgers the trick usually build a fire around the tree and burn all the swarm."

"If you don't mind, I'd rather let some bear get the honey. Bears somehow don't mind getting stung. The next time the Indians demand a shilling for a quart of honey, I won't begrudge them the money."

❧

Margo also delighted in watching the birds, especially the parakeets, which were numerous and very tame. She had never seen any bird with such lovely coloring. She made Gabriel promise never to shoot any of them. He agreed readily to the request. They would not be worth the powder and shot. But this was not so in the case of the passenger pigeons, which made a very generous serving.

One day the whole sky darkened as a thick cloud arrived and there appeared to be a light snow. Margo soon saw that the cloud consisted of millions of passenger pigeons and what appeared to be snow was their droppings. The birds were so thick she could not see the sky beyond them, and from time to time an exhausted bird fell dead nearby. Except for the dead birds on the ground, the entire flock flew on, leaving a bright blue sky behind them.

I wonder, Margo asked herself, where they will land. If they perch as thickly as they are flying, they will strip all the branches off the trees, and they certainly won't find enough to eat. Margo would not have believed that both the parakeets and the passenger pigeons would be extinct in less than two centuries.

Margo also loved watching the wood ducks, which were called summer ducks because they remained behind after the mallards and teal went north.

"These beautiful birds eat mostly acorns and nest in hollow trees," Gabriel said.

"Just look at that tiny little ruby-throated humming bird, not much larger than a bumble bee. When I get home I'm going to hang out a feeder full of honey water the way Mrs. Milledge does."

∼

One evening Margo asked Mrs. Milledge, "How did people learn the names of all these flowers and birds?" By then her English had greatly improved.

"We usually just use the name of the most similar plant or creature found in England," Mrs. Milledge answered, or else we ask the Indians and write what we think we hear."

The conversation took an abrupt turn when Margo remarked, "It's such a calm and clear evening, why is there so much distant thunder?"

"That's not thunder," Gabriel explained, "it's bull alligators bellowing. Let's go over to Catesby's Swamp and watch some of them."

After a half mile ride the couple reached the area where the alligators were roaring, and there they saw two of the bulls in mortal combat. An exciting spectacle as the huge beasts tore at each other, each grasping the other's legs in its powerful tooth-studded jaws. Finally, one of the fighters, badly mauled, slunk away in shame. Margo was shaken by the violence and clung to Gabriel.

"Do you know who man's best friend is?" Gabriel asked.

"The dog, of course, like Kumpan."

"No," he corrected her. "The male alligator."

"Why is that?" Margo asked, expecting something unexpected.

"Well, you see. A female alligator eats a few snapping turtles or perhaps a hound or two and then climbs up a mud bank, digs a hole, drops a couple of dozen eggs into it, and covers it over. Then, after she has stilled her appetite on a deer or hog or whatnot she digs another hole and fills it with eggs, too. Fortunately for us, a male alligator usually follows her, digs up the nests, and eats most of the eggs. If he didn't, we'd be waist deep in alligators."

Margo did not like being teased, especially when she could not think of a suitable comeback.

∼

On their next excursion together Gabriel took three oversized fish hooks made for him by the smith in Ebenezer. He also bought a heavy piece of steel wire and twelve feet of rope. Margo refrained from asking questions until Gabriel shot a blue heron, something she had never seen him do.

"Why did you shoot that poor bird? You know they are not worth eating."

"You'll see," Gabriel replied, impaling the bird on the three hooks. He then picked out a sturdy bough hanging out over the bank of a swampy stream and suspended the heron just above the water with its feet dangling as if it were standing on floating grass.

"Let's get going," Gabriel ordered, without accounting for his unusual actions.

When the couple returned to the spot late in the evening, an immense alligator was thrashing the water violently and sending spray in all directions. The large reptile had jumped up in the air to catch the heron and had become snagged on the hooks. Gabriel shot the mammoth saurian between the eyes, pulled it ashore, cut off the last three feet of its tail, and recovered his tackle. Turning off the trail, he rode to a temporary camp of some migrant Creek hunters and told them where they could find the rest of the alligator.

"How did you think up that trap?" Margo asked.

"I didn't. It's a wolf hook. Been used for centuries in Europe, and can be used for foxes, too."

That night Gabriel, Margo, Kumpan, and Panzer ate barbecued alligator steaks. They were delicious, like lean beef and flavored with Gabriel's very best spices, gifts from his Indian friends. The next night Gabriel prepared the entrée himself.

"Very tasty," Margo congratulated the cook. "What is it?"

"Fillet of rattlesnake," was the proud answer.

～

Returning to Fort Argyle one brisk day, the sergeant and his wife dallied en route and had to stop for the night. Gabriel turned off into an inconspicuous trail leading into a dense cassina and myrtle thicket. Mak-

87

ing a spiral, they passed close along the path they had just covered. At a cleared spot they tethered their horses and left Kumpan and Panzer to sleep on a blanket. Then, taking their rations from their saddle bags, they proceeded on foot, crouching down under the dense foliage until they came upon a lean-to in a small clearing. Gabriel had arranged this secluded camp site, from which he could spy on any intruders following the trail, while keeping an eye on his horse. Here Gabriel could sleep the sleep of the just, with no danger of hostile Indians sneaking up on him.

"This is my secret hideaway," Gabriel confided. "More or less midway between all my destinations." He then recovered a large canvas bag that had been carefully concealed in the shrubbery. From it he removed two blankets and a flask of peach brandy.

Margo was preoccupied with a chameleon, which was crossing her green skirt and was taking on its hue. When the lizard reached her leather jacket, it assumed a brown color before pouncing on a blue-bottled fly that had just landed there. Chameleons are like people, she mused, able to change color. Why do I always draw some moral conclusion from everything? Perhaps because I'm Swiss?

Seeing the magnolia tree overhead and the many flowers blooming in the grass, Margo recalled a little folksong she had learned back home. She sang the well-rhymed verses in her rich contralto voice:

> Under the linden on the heath,
> that is where we had our bed,
> where flowers and grass are crushed.
> Before a forest in a vale,
> Tarandadei,
> so sweetly sang a nightingale.
>
> I came awalking to the meadow
> where my love had come before
> and made a bed of blossoms.
> Did he kiss me? A thousand times!
> Tarandadei,

See how red my mouth is!

If anyone comes along the path,
he will have a hearty laugh
when from the flowers he will see
where my head was lying.
Tarandadei,
So sweetly sang the nightingale.

If anyone knew he was lying with me
(May God forbid!), I'd be ashamed.
What he did with me may no one discover
but him and me and the little bird,
Tarandadei,
Who may well keep our little secret!

"To be sure," Margo conceded, "the little bird in the song is a nightingale, but I'll settle any day for a mocking bird. When it's not imitating the ugly sounds of other birds, it sings just as beautifully as any nightingale I've ever heard. And I would just as soon have a magnolia tree as a linden tree even if it's not in bloom."

Margo was interrupted by the sound of falling objects.

"What's that noise?"

"Seed pods are falling from the magnolia tree," Gabriel answered, picking up one of the odd-looking fruits. "The magnolia may have no blossoms at this time of year, but at least it has these crimson pods."

Soon after finishing her song, Margo saw that Gabriel was hungering for her, even dropping his eyelids to half mast. She had never made love in the open but knew that it was often done, as in her song of love under the linden tree. Although irresistibly drawn to Gabriel, she resolved not to leave him in total command as usual. She resented the fact that, whenever she was overcome by unbridled passion, he seemed so very controlled. She still remembered the night when the Schneider women interrupted them. While she was lost to the world in complete surrender, he was calm and collected as he threw the covers over her and climbed out of the back window.

Heidi, the girl from whom Margo had learned her song about the tryst under the linden, was more advanced sexually than the other sixteen-year-olds in the village. She even understood and trusted the calendar, and it was rumored that she had experimented with several of the village boys. The other girls did not dare. If a girl got pregnant, only two possible consequences: the boy would marry her, perhaps reluctantly, or else he would enlist in the military to escape her parents, leaving her a social outcast and a disgrace to her family. A neighboring village was said to have a constant population. Every time a man left town a baby was born.

Among the things the liberated girl had told Margo was that, whereas a woman's most erotic zone was her lips, a man's was his tongue. Strange, Margo reflected, that I've never had a deep kiss. Stout hardly kissed me at all. Gabriel is an inventive lover, he has kissed my hands, eyes, earlobes, nape, throat, and breasts; but we have never rubbed tongues. Perhaps he thinks I would consider it offensive.

Later, when Gabriel took her in his arms and placed his lips firmly on hers, she parted her lips and teeth and teased his tongue. A violent jolt coursed through his body, and she knew he was truly sharing her swirling sensations. His tongue then sought out the hidden recesses of her mouth. They both undressed as far as necessary, knowing that the mocking bird would keep their secret. From now on they would always play on a more level field, now that she had discovered his Achilles heel. She was sure Azuki never inspired such a response.

~

On the way back to Fort Argyle, Panzer was again perched on Pegasus's back while Kumpan ranged in large circles. All at once Kumpan flushed a doe which, confused, ran toward Pegasus. Panzer sprang to the ground, made three or four long jumps, and leaped with all claws unsheathed onto the back of the doe, which she killed quickly with one bite on her neck.

"How dreadful of our gentle little Panzer!" Margo exclaimed.

90

"Just following her instincts," Gabriel said. "She didn't need any mother to teach her what to do."

As usual, Gabriel disemboweled the doe for Kumpan and Panzer and then wrapped her body in a sheet of waxed linen to keep her blood from getting on Pegasus and his accoutrements. The next day Panzer was not to be found. She had come of age and no longer needed support.

"Possibly she smelled a mate," Gabriel suggested. He remembered having recently heard a lovesick panther screeching in the forest.

～

A few days later Gabriel was ordered to take a dispatch to Purysburg. "Why don't you come along for the ride? We are expecting excellent weather. A good chance for you to meet Azuki."

Margo froze. What brought on this confrontation? How am I to act? Will I be in a command position, or will I just be the guest? Is Gabriel going to come to some decision? Margo pondered over all this, and the ride went with almost no conversation. A long and dreary trip, the fog was gloomy. No birds were singing, and no flowers were in bloom.

"What's the matter? Did a crow get your tongue?"

"No, just a bit tired."

Margo tried to keep up idle chatter, but her heart was not in it. The miles passed slowly until they finally came upon a small cabin in an immaculately swept yard of white sand. Azuki ran out to meet her guests and greeted them with a toothless smile. She proudly showed Gabriel six more hides that she had tanned since his last visit. Quite a feat for a ninety-three year old woman!

"The best leather worker in the colony," Gabriel informed Margo. "She prepares all my deer and beaver skins." He groped around in his saddlebags and took out a jar of sugar as a present for Azuki and a sack of salt for curing hides. "Azuki, this is my squaw, Margo." Azuki mumbled something through her toothless gums.

"Very, very pleased to meet you," Margo said. She was telling God's truth. On Margo's return journey, the sun was shining, the birds were singing, and the flowers were in bloom.

Upon their arrival at Fort Argyle, Margo found all in order, but three days later her cow Liesel did not return from pasture at the customary hour. Margo's neighbor, who had been milking Liesel in her owner's absence, assured Margo that she always returned when expected. Since Gabriel and Kumpan had just gone on a mission, Margo could not send Kumpan to find the missing animal, so she set out alone for Liesel's favorite pasturage. There she found her cow dying of a gunshot wound. The hide and beef had not been taken. Only her bell was missing. Some Indian had killed her just for her bell, not knowing that he could have approached the friendly beast and taken the bell without hurting her. Although truly saddened, Margo, being Swiss and practical, had someone salvage the hide and beef.

$\sim$

When Gabriel's troop was transferred from Fort Argyle to Fort Frederica, he and several other men rode the horses to the shore opposite St. Simons, having to ford or swim several rivers way upstream. Most of the remaining garrison and their families and all their belongings were loaded into petiaguas and other craft, including Jones' scout boat, and taken down to the mouth of the Ogeechee at Hell's Gate, and then via the inland water route to St. Simons.

"What kind of cannon is that?," Margo asked a brawny, grey-bearded rower.

"It's a swivel gun. It can throw a three-pound shot, or three pounds of grape. That's enough to blow any canoe out of the water. Besides that, it can shoot twice as far as any musket, so we ain't afeared of no Indians attacking us by daylight. Jones practically controls the entire inland water route from Thunderbolt to Saint Simons."

At Frederica, as the wife of a celebrated sergeant, Margo enjoyed more prestige than she had ever had before. Most of Savannah's able-bodied men as well as the South Carolina regiment were stationed there, and Frederica now had a much larger population than Savannah. War was Georgia's chief business. Everyone was in service or furnishing labor or supplies.

Near Frederica was the encampment of Oglethorpe's Indian allies, who came to town frequently to receive their gifts and get drunk.

"Who's in command of these Indians?" Margo asked.

"Captain Jones," a statuesque woman answered, balancing a large basket on her head.

"Not Noble Jones?"

"No, Capt. Thomas Jones, a half-caste trader, who is not to be confused with Capt. Noble Jones. And don't confuse him with Mr. Thomas Jones, Causton's successor, either." Causton, the previous keeper of the stores, had returned to London to justify some irregularities in his accounts. Jealous people had noted that his plantation, Oxstead, was far better built and maintained than any other one in Georgia.

Sometimes Margo would go to the Indians' encampment to watch their dances. She had missed the busk, or harvest dance; but now was the time for almost continuous war dances. The warriors, with gaudily painted faces, danced to deafening drums and war cries and proclaimed and re-enacted their individual feats of arms. This really served little purpose, since all the braves were boasting at the same time and no one was listening. Everyone, including the female spectators, were wildly drunk.

Having heard lurid details of the massacre at Fort Mount Venture, Margo asked her husband, "Are the English Indians really any more humane than the Spanish Indians?"

"Of course they are! We have told them to spare all women and children."

"And how do you know whether a scalp is from a man or a woman? I don't think we should buy scalps from the Indians. Suppose one of those we bought was that of Mrs. Francis? Why can't the English and Spanish agree not to buy any more scalps?" This was a question the English and Spanish authorities themselves could not answer.

～

"Have you heard about the murder of the two Highlanders on Amelia Island?" Gabriel's lean corporal Lightner asked, clearing his throat and arranging his hair.

"Not yet."

"Both were suffering from dysentery and had withdrawn into the

93

bush to relieve themselves. Some Spanish Indians scalped and killed them and cut off their balls."

Gabriel suspected that this was the same war party that had murdered Lieutenant Francis' family. Having a Florida Indian among his guides, he sent him to visit the war party, which was then camped near Saint Augustine. There the spy heard the warriors boasting of the scalps they had taken on both occasions. Gabriel also learned that the chief of the party was named Esteechy, a name he engraved on his heart.

Some weeks later Margo heard that a war party allied to the British had just returned from Florida and was going to perform a victory dance. As she neared the dancing braves she thought she smelled a barbecue. Odd, because there had been no food at the other occasions. As she came closer, she saw what she thought was a pig being roasted.

It was not a pig. It was a man. He was so charred that Margo could not tell whether he was an Indian or a white man. He seemed to be unconscious. A squaw approached with a bucket of cold water and poured it on him so the fun could begin all over again. Suddenly a wrenching roar of pain. Margo vomited and fled from the scene.

～

At Frederica, Margo and Gabriel were allotted one of the soldier huts, a simple shelter covered with palmetto branches that gave some protection from the sun and rain but not from the cold.

"These shacks were designed by a Jew from Brazil," their civilian neighbor informed them. "Oglethorpe sent him down from Savannah to show us how to build them."

"What are the floor and fireplace made of?" Margo asked, tapping them with her shoe.

"They're made of tabby, baked clay, and oyster shells," the neighbor replied. "There's no shortage of shells because there are large mounds of them around here left by generations of oyster-eating Indians. Oglethorpe gives credit to a Swiss here named Heinrich Meyer for finding a better way to make tabby." Meyer was the father of the disrespectful young Heinrich Meyer of Old Ebenezer and also of Magdalena, the girl debauched by Wilhelm Taescher.

94

The palmetto huts were all identical and laid out regularly on parallel streets. Around the settlement was a high stockade with a tower at each corner. The square fort, made of masonry, had an arrowhead-shaped bastion at each corner from which the garrison could cover the ditch and embankment with flanking fire. Pointing to the bastions, Gabriel explained, "Samuel Augspurger, the Swiss surveyor and engineer who designed the fort, was a disciple of the French military engineer Vauban. As a result, there is no way a person can reach the palisade without coming under fire." Although a cavalryman at heart, Gabriel was interested in all things military.

∿

What Margo enjoyed most at Frederica were the orange groves, from which she was free to pick as many oranges as she wished.

"Except for the ones Stout brought me from the Trustees' Garden," she told Gabriel, "I saw only one orange in all my life. I've told you how, when I was grazing my goats on an alpine meadow, some quality folk arrived in a gilded coach to have a picnic. Well, while the servants were packing up to go home, one of the ladies gave me an orange. It must have been grown in an orangery, or green house, because no oranges grow in the open in Switzerland. The orange was so beautiful I refrained from eating it. Instead I saved it and showed it to all the village children until it was so dried out and shriveled up that it was no longer any good."

∿

What Margo missed most at Frederica were Richard and Frances, who had so well assuaged her grief for her two little brothers while she was at Savannah and again Fort Argyle. On her third day at Fort Frederica she chanced to see three children of similar ages playing ball. When the older boy threw a ball to his little sister, she missed and the ball rolled to Margo's feet. She picked up the ball and threw it back to the older boy, who caught it with a great show of pride. She joined in the game and quickly won the children's confidence.

"Who are those darling children?" she asked a young naval officer after their mother called them home.

"They belong to Captain Horton, who is commanding officer here in Oglethorpe's absence. He's the tall fellow with the bright red beard." Margo wondered why, with the exception of a few ancient greybeards, the only full beards she had seen, those of Wiggins, McPherson, and Horton, were all bright red.

The next morning, well groomed, Margo called on Mrs. Horton to ask whether she could use a domestic servant.

"Gracious Lady, I recommend me to you." Margo had translated this directly from the German.

Before Mrs. Horton could answer, her children crowded around Margo and asked her to play ball with them again. The two women came to terms quickly: Margo was to care for the children and see to their clothes and laundry and also attend Captain Horton's elderly and lonesome mother. And, best of all, she was given a large private room, in which Gabriel could stay with her on his infrequent leaves in those turbulent times.

Margo was delighted to have the children, Benjamin, Harold, and Elsbeth, who were about the ages of her little brothers before the tragedy on the *Europa*. One of her most enjoyable duties was telling the children their bedtime stories. She told them *Sleeping Beauty*, *Goldilocks*, and *Cinderella*, all with great success despite her still limited vocabulary and outlandish accent. Then she told them the story about Iwain, basing it on the brief outline given by Gabriel.

This tale was so well received that the children asked to hear it again the very next evening. Before she had proceeded very far into the story the second time, Margo noticed she had lost her audience. An embarrassing pause. Finally, Benjamin, as spokesman, said, "But you are telling it wrong. It wasn't a white horse. It was a black horse." The other two children nodded in agreement, wanting the story to be told correctly.

Margo apologetically corrected her grievous error and then tried strenuously to tell the tale exactly as she had told it the previous evening. She must have succeeded, because there were no more corrections. Then and there Margo determined never to repeat a story. She might use the very same events and the very same princes, princesses, giants, and dragons, but every story would be an original the children had not yet heard.

Margo enjoyed entertaining the children, but she would have preferred entertaining some of her own. At least she was getting practice for the future.

To help Margo in her story telling and game organizing, the young Mrs. Horton taught her to play several little tunes on her pianoforte. Margo did not stop there, she began playing little melodies she had learned as a child. With some help from Mrs. Horton she learned to read the notes to the songs and hymns she knew, and within the year she could pass as a fair pianist.

～

Margo enjoyed entertaining the elderly grandmother, who was very talkative.

"You are really making progress," the old lady assured Margo. "You are rapidly mastering the King's English."

"Thank you, Ma'am."

"Never talk with the soldiers or their Cockney wives, or they will corrupt your fine speech."

"I'll remember," Margo promised.

Although the Swiss engineer Augspurger was very cordial and wished keenly to talk with Margo in their shared Bernese dialect, she preferred speaking only English, the key to rising in American society. Margo also found opportunities to talk with Mrs. Raymond Demere, one of the few educated women on the island. Speaking English only with gentlewomen, Margo gradually began to sound like one herself when she spoke English, yet she was still a village maid when she spoke her native Swiss dialect.

I must never tell my English friends I can't read or write. They assume I just don't know the English alphabet, which I am sure they will gladly teach me. Margo was right, they did so, and she quickly learned to write English with a bold and flowery hand. She greatly preferred the simple English script to the fancy German letters that had always seemed so intimidating. Gabriel being away most of the time, Margo's English made rapid progress.

～

Margo's greatest discovery was the realm of books. Being lonesome herself, the senior Mrs. Horton took a fancy to the young woman and chatted with her about the outside world, of which Margo knew so woefully little. While Margo could now speak intelligible English, she mispronounced most words she came across first when reading. Mrs. Horton went to great lengths to help her master spelling idiosyncracies such as bough, cough, rough, though, and through. She even taught her to pronounce the English *th*, which she and Gabriel had never mastered.

"Keep a list of all new words you learn, and memorize them every night." Mrs. Horton let Margo read to her for hours on end and corrected all her many mispronunciations until she acquired the complete vocabulary of all the old lady's romances. In time Margo became so familiar with the world of polite fiction that she felt she belonged in a fashionable parlor rather than at a remote and isolated fortress; and she began to realize that she was rapidly leaving Gabriel's world. The old lady even amused herself by having her young Galatea alter and wear some of her own now out-of-date dresses and carry her parasol.

∾

One afternoon a serving girl asked Margo, "Have you heard about the privateer from Rhode Island?"

"No, tell me."

"It's just made port with a captured Spanish merchantman full of merchandise for Mexico. Wishing to get back to sea to capture a treasure ship, the privateer captain sold the entire cargo to Major Horton, who paid a fraction of its true value. There are still some bargains, but at steep mark-up."

Margo hurried to the sale. Among the objects she found a peacock feather fan, which she bought in order to put its plumes on an old hat Mrs. Horton had given her. She also bought a hunting knife for Gabriel, a true Toledo blade.

∾

Chief among Margo's pleasures in Frederica was walking along the waterfront and enjoying the bright sunlight, which she had scarcely seen as long as they were incarcerated under the thick roof of pine and cypress tops around Fort Argyle. Most delightful were the splendid sunsets over the vast golden marshes across Frederica River. But even there she could see only as far as the horizon. As a child, while grazing her sheep and goats on the Hoernli, she could see the Matterhorn so clearly that she could almost reach out and touch it. It was ninety miles away.

One morning Margo saw an exciting spectacle. An osprey, one of many, swooped down and caught a large fish; but, before it could find a roosting place to eat its prey, a bald eagle came from nowhere. The osprey tried to escape the larger bird, but that was impossible, especially because of its heavy booty. Giving up the struggle, the osprey shrieked in anger and dropped the fish. The eagle waited aloft until the fish had fallen half way to the water, then it stooped and caught the fish just before it hit the surface. As the eagle carried away its prize, Margo asked a fisherman, who was watching the contest,

"Does the eagle ever catch a fish for himself?"

"Not as I ever seed," the old salt answered. "I spose he coulda catched one ifn he wanted to, but I reckon that, as king of the birds, he's just taking what's owed him."

During her subsequent walks along the river Margo saw eagles rob ospreys several times without ever seeing one catch a fish for itself. I suppose, Margo concluded, the bird kingdom is like the human kingdom, the winnings go to the strongest. The European aristocrats, Margo remembered, often name their castles for birds of prey. Many castles have names referring to eagles, hawks, and falcons, but none referring to doves and nightingales.

∽

As Margo perfected her English and chatted easily with the British officers and their ladies, Gabriel gradually began to feel left out. He saw that his wife was weary of hearing only about Kumpan, Pegasus, Panzer, and Indians and that the self-made intellectual preferred discussing subjects unfamiliar to him. Margo tried to share some of her newly acquired knowledge with him, but Gabriel was unreceptive, being a spontaneous but unlettered man. He had never read a real book, nor did he intend to. He, too, was gradually realizing that they had little in common but their bed. The Hortons tried to make Gabriel feel at home, but somehow he was never entirely at ease under their roof, in part because of his non-commissioned status. He resented the expression "Officers and their ladies" as opposed to "Enlisted men and their wives." He considered Margo as much a lady as any colonel's wife.

8

War of Jenkin's Ear

Meanwhile, Oglethorpe was planning a show-down with the Spaniards.

"Almost all the able-bodied men and boys at Savannah are in military training," Gabriel's chubby corporal Rowner reported with his staccato stutter, "except for the Moravians." Rowner always seemed to get the news before anyone else.

"I hear the people in Savannah are angry at the Trustees for exempting the Moravians from military service," Corporal Lightner said, having cleared his throat portentously.

"They would make very sorry soldiers," Corporal Rowner judged, stuttering this time less than usual. "They are much more valuable on the home front. They are the most industrious and skilled artisans we have. And the cheapest."

"That's because they only demand Christian wages," Margo added.

"And what are Christian wages?" Gabriel asked.

"According to Boltzius, Christian wages are what one needs to keep one alive in one's divinely appointed condition," Margo explained. "To demand more would reveal greed and vanity." This ran counter to Margo's secret dream of the Gilded Coach.

The Moravians live communally," Gabriel said, "and most of them have no children. That's why they can work so cheap."

"And that's the reason our working men resent them so much," Lightner contributed, clearing his throat. "If they are exempted from military service, everyone else will claim the same privilege."

"They say that the Swiss planter Peter Morel is drilling all the men at Vernonburg and Highfield," another added.

"He's the right man for the job. He can command in both German and French."

Margo listened avidly to all these conversations and tried to form her own opinions.

~

Jacob Roeck, a hard-drinking Purysburg shoemaker, visited Ebenezer to recruit soldiers for a Carolina regiment that was to participate in the four-month campaign against St. Augustine. Even though the Protestant Salzburgers would surely be expelled from their homes again if the Catholic Spaniards conquered Georgia, Boltzius dissuaded all his Salzburgers from volunteering. Being from Prussia, a land frequently ravaged by war, he disapproved of military service.

"Righteous people do not let themselves be used for this purpose," he pontificated, "but rather those who like to roam around and find pleasure in such a dissolute life. Besides that, the campaign won't be just four months, as promised; and it may not succeed." Daringly, Boltzius pronounced these seditious words right during Oglethorpe's visit at Ebenezer.

While failing to recruit any true Salzburgers, Roeck did succeed in enlisting some ten of their indentured Palatine servants by promising that, by serving just four months, they could free themselves from the indentured labor they still owed. The men who could ride were assigned to a cavalry troop that Gabriel was then organizing at Fort Argyle.

"Why have only two of the ten volunteers from Ebenezer chosen cavalry service?," Milledge asked. "Didn't they ever hear horsemen sing 'If you want to have a good time, jine the cavalry'?"

"In Europe few peasants can ride," Gabriel answered the captain. "They usually walk while leading their plow and cart horses, which are mostly geldings and mares. The nobles discourage their peasantry from riding, since they owe their superior status to their monopoly of war horses and to their skill in riding."

~

During Oglethorpe's feverish military buildup at Frederica, Gabriel's troop was on constant intelligence and counter-intelligence missions.

"Men," Gabriel ordered, "our job is to learn whatever we can about the movements of the Spaniards and their Indians while denying them knowledge of British activities at Frederica. Understood?"

"Aye, aye, Sir."

"In this we will be much helped by Noble Jones and his 'Georgia Marines' in their scout boat. It can ferry two men at a time with their horses." Although recently promoted to captain of the Rangers, Jones still skippered the scout boat. He was a jack of all trades and mastered many.

While Gabriel was reconnoitering some terrain near the Saint John's River one cloudy day, Corporal Lightner pointed down the path.

"Sergeant, about two hundred yards down the trail," Lightner said, without clearing his voice. "On the left, in front of the tall cypress tree."

"I don't see anything," Gabriel whispered, looking through his field glass.

"At the foot of the second cypress."

Gabriel focussed his field glass again and discerned a man in Spanish uniform signalling to them furtively to go back. Focussing his glass more carefully, he saw the soldier was black. Then he recognized him as the runaway slave he had freed near Fort Argyle. To show his gratitude, the liberated slave was saving Gabriel and his troop from a well-laid ambush. Gabriel made a quick pirouette and led his men to safety.

～

Believing his forces adequate to capture Saint Augustine, Oglethorpe marched them to the Saint Johns River, where he easily captured two small Spanish outposts. But then things began to go awry. The weather became unbearably hot, and fever broke out in all ranks. Also, disagreements and incriminations occurred between the South Carolinians and the Georgians, and this gave the Spaniards time to call in their outlying forces and to supply the city to withstand a siege.

"Did you hear about Fort Moosa?" a one-eyed sailor asked Margo.

"No, what's that?"

"A fortified building close to Saint Augustine," the jack-tar answered. "The Highlanders captured it from its black garrison in a really rough fight."

"And then?"

"Unexpectedly, the expelled garrison, reinforced by other black troops, counterattacked and killed or captured all the Highlanders in the fort. Oglethorpe claims he lost only a dozen men, but there were far more lost than that."

To make matters even worse, a sandbar prevented Oglethorpe's supporting warships from coming close enough to bombard the fort, and his field artillery was far too inadequate to subdue it. Realizing that he could not take the heavily fortified city by storm, Oglethorpe had to lay siege.

"It's a strange thing," Gabriel remarked. "Usually a city under siege can be starved out, but here the besieged city has enough provisions while it's the besiegers who are starving. Besides that, yesterday some supply ships from Havana slipped right through our blockade."

Eventually, sickness so thinned Oglethorpe's ranks that he had to abandon the siege and return with his sick and weary troops to Frederica to await a Spanish counterattack. The Carolina troops beat a hasty retreat to Charleston.

"Oglethorpe is entirely responsible for the debacle," the Carolinians swore.

～

During these tragic weeks, Gabriel was kept busy finding lost and sick stragglers and saving them from the scalp-hungry Indians. After a skirmish with some Spanish Indians, Gabriel had the satisfaction of recognizing Esteechy, who had massacred the people at Fort Mount Pleasant as well as the two Highlanders. Gabriel turned the man over to his own Indians for proper disposal. This was a dire error.

～

The siege of Saint Augustine having failed, Gabriel returned to Frederica and began to share Margo's life and bed. With so many people at Frederica, food had become very dear. Bread and wine were out of the question for all but the highest ranking officers and leading merchants; but sometimes the industrious Abraham Minis, now one of Oglethorpe's chief purveyors, would let Margo have some goods at reasonable rates.

"I understand," Minis said, "that the high price of real beer is going to drop, now that Captain Horton has established his brewery and planted a successful crop of hops on his plantation on Jeckyll Island."

Someone else added, "I understand that Horton is suffering competition from the Salzburgers' peach brandy, which the enterprising Maria Barbara Roth is importing from Ebenezer."

The chief source of wealth in Georgia at the time was the pay of Oglethorpe's soldiers, and he wished to keep all currency circulating in the colony by encouraging as much local production as possible.

~

Despite the social graces the older Mrs. Horton had taught her, Margo was not too proud to make do with little.

"You won't have to buy any more wheat flour and coffee, now that they are so expensive," she told the younger Mrs. Horton. "I can make hoe cakes from cornmeal and coffee from parched corn kernels. I can also brew small beer from molasses and Indian corn, and I can brew tea from cassina leaves." She had learned all these primitive skills already at Fort Argyle.

Since the salted beef imported from Ireland for the soldiers was unpalatable, Margo bought meat at the "butcher shop", a stump where farmers sold beef and Indians sold game. Sometimes Gabriel brought back wild turkeys or venison from his patrols. Also, fish were free for the taking. In Georgia everyone had the right to catch as many fish as he needed.

"Eat those nasty oysters?" Margo objected, never having seen one before. "I'd just as soon eat worms!" But Margo was flexible, and with much will power she finally ate one, holding her nose as she did so. After overcoming her initial repugnance, Margo actually became fond of oysters, which literally grew on trees. She and her new friends would build a large fire and place a sheet of iron over the coals. Then they would pour a bushel or two of oysters on it, cover them with damp Spanish moss, and wait until the oysters willingly opened their shells. Spanish moss, which hung from the trees like long grey beards, was also burned in pots as smudges to keep away the gnats.

"Which would you prefer tonight, Gabriel, my Love?" Margo would often ask, "to be strangled by smoke or devoured by gnats?" Mosquito nets were far too expensive to consider. Margo started knitting one herself but realized that it would take years.

Life at Frederica became more and more oppressive. The Spaniards were going to counterattack, but no one knew where or when. Wild rumors were making the rounds.

"I heard that the governor of Cuba is already on the way with seven thousand troops and eighty sails," young Mrs. Horton reported.

"I see that all the merchants have evacuated the city with their wares. Soon there won't be any food to eat," Mrs. Demere predicted.

～

Less than a year after Oglethorpe's unsuccessful siege of Saint Augustine, the governor of Cuba was ready for his counterattack, bringing almost as many ships and men as the wildest rumors had foretold. Oglethorpe was undaunted. He was everywhere at once, encouraging his men, calling in outlying troops, and ordering his armed sloops and other vessels to fight their way to Frederica through the Spanish blockade. The sailors were disembarked to serve as soldiers. The harried general ordered all his troops on St. Simons back to Frederica, while the Spaniards landed several thousand men at the south end of the island.

Gabriel's patrol was monitoring the large Spanish force as it approached Frederica along the military road from the southern tip of the island.

"What do you think Oglethorpe will do?" he asked Lightner.

"He'll fight, that's what he'll do," the corporal answered in his bass voice. "I know the Spaniards have ten times as many men," the lanky trooper boasted, "but our men are rearing to fight. The General will let the Spaniards get close to Frederica, but not to it."

Gabriel was pleased with this answer, which expressed the general morale. Gabriel's patrol was the first to make contact with the two Spanish units moving up the military road and now converging into a single colorful column. He had his men fire one volley before retiring, then he sent his two fastest riders to carry the alarm to Frederica. Slowly withdrawing for a mile, he found Oglethorpe preparing an ambush.

"Look over there," Gabriel said, pointing and handing his field glass to Lightner. "Do you see the Spanish army's advance guard debouching from the forest onto the marsh? Over to the left. They're are stopping to catch a breath." His words were suddenly drowned by gunfire. The Highlanders, who had been carefully concealed behind the brush along the edge of the marsh, opened a disastrous fire. Panic and confusion reigned among the Spaniards. Some returned fire into the woods from which the bullets were coming; but, being unaimed, this fusillade accomplished little. Others tried to help their wounded friends or else ran for their lives.

A few tried to form ranks, but that was made difficult because so many officers were missing, either hit by British bullets or retreating headlong into the woods. The British then pursued the Spaniards almost to the south end of the island where they had landed and where they were protected by naval gunfire.

Gabriel's troop captured four of the fleeing Spaniards and shot two who would not surrender. Only two of his men were wounded, none killed.

～

Danger was not over for Oglethorpe. His losses had been minimal, but the Spaniards on Saint Simons still outnumbered his men ten to one. He prepared energetically for the next assault. It never came.

"Why didn't the Spaniards attack again?" Rowner asked in his high voice two days after the skirmish. Somehow he controlled his stammer.

"I heard Oglethorpe forged a letter and let it fall into the hands of the Spaniards," Lightner answered, again rearranging his sparce hair. "The letter said Oglethorpe just needed to hold out a day or two more, and then a rescue fleet would arrive with a strong army. They say some of the Spanish officers thought it a hoax, but others thought it true."

"Good for them!" Margo exclaimed, clapping her hands.

"In any case, the attack has been called off," Lightner resumed in his deep voice "and the Spanish army has retreated to the south end of Saint Simons and is taking ship back to St. Augustine."

"This was not the first time Oglethorpe tricked the Spaniards," a youthful midshipman joined in. "When he first built the fort at Frederica he invited Moral de Sanchez . . ."

"Moral de who?" Margo asked.

"The governor at Saint Augustine. Oglethorpe invited him to come and negotiate with him. As the Spaniards' boat came up the winding Frederica river, it passed many clearings in the forest, in each of which was a smartly drawn up troop of sixty to eighty men, who fired several cannons in the visitor's honor. The Spanish governor was very discouraged at seeing such a large force, at least four times as many as he had expected. He did not know that it was the same troop with the same cannons at each clearing."

~

With the miraculous withdrawal of the enemy, everyone at Frederica could breathe again; and the merchants and many of the refugees began returning from Savannah, Purysburg, and Ebenezer. Oglethorpe proclaimed a day of thanksgiving to God for the victory, much to the pleasure of Boltzius and the pious Colonel Stephens.

Gabriel remained with Margo for a week before taking a dispatch to Port Royal via Fort Argyle and Purysburg. During the great buildup at Frederica, Fort Argyle had been all but abandoned; and all the civilians had departed. The old fort was now occupied only by a caretaker and his wife.

When Gabriel and his patrol reached Fort Argyle, they found the caretaker and his wife murdered.

"This wasn't done by Indians," Gabriel concluded. "Indians always scalp, they never decapitate. The murderers must have been white guests who killed their hosts for their money."

"To judge by the freshness of the blood," Corporal Rowner stuttered, "they must have departed only a few hours ago." It had rained all night, and the only hoof prints led in the direction of Mount Pleasant. Gabriel set a fast pace in order to catch the culprits before they crossed the ferry.

Several hours later Gabriel and his two Rangers were in sight of Mount Pleasant. Smoke wafted from a lean-to, in front of which two horses were tied. Sending Rowner to outflank the quarry, Gabriel and Lightner stepped up to the open side of the lean-to and aimed their pistols at the two occupants.

"Hands up in the name of the King!" Gabriel commanded. Unarmed, the two men complied. Gabriel saw two pistols in a belt hanging on the back of the door. He thought he recognized one of the men.

"Are you Dr. Mazzique?" he asked.

"Yes, I am."

"Did you kill the caretakers at Fort Argyle?"

"Yes we did," Mazzique admitted.

Gabriel did not deign to speak to the younger man, whom he recognized as William Shannon, one of the Irishmen redeemed by Oglethorpe.

"Why did you decapitate your victims?" Gabriel asked. "Everyone knows the Indians scalp, rather than decapitate, so the blame could not be put on them."

"But runaway blacks do decapitate," the doctor said. "There was a party of them in the neighborhood who might have been held responsible." Gabriel had never once thought of that possibility. The prisoners were securely bound. Soon thereafter a petiagua loaded with deer skins landed at Mount Pleasant so the crew could cook a meal.

"Will you please take the prisoners down to Savannah with you?" Gabriel asked the boatmen. "Rowner, accompany them with the loot as Crown evidence."

In two days the culprits were tried, and the very next day they were hanged. Mazzique, claiming to be a Protestant, was buried in holy ground. Shannon was hung on a gibbet at the mouth of the Ogeechee River as a warning to other would-be robbers, and the location received the name Shannon's Point.

~

Gabriel and Lightner began their way back toward Purysburg leading the two captured horses. After they had gone only a few miles shots rang out and both of them were struck. They fired simultaneously at an Indian sniper in a tree, who fell to earth with a resounding crash.

"Pegasus, make a fast pirouette," Gabriel ordered with his voice and his heels. Other Indians fired at the two wounded riders but missed when the horsemen made their rapid about-face and started back in the direction of Fort Argyle. Kumpan was not so lucky. He was killed in the fusillade while hanging on an Indian's throat. Gabriel had not expected any Yemassee Indians so far north after the Spanish defeat at Bloody Marsh. He had not foreseen a retaliation by Esteechy's kinsmen.

Gabriel was bleeding profusely from a wound in the chest. Lightner mounted Pegasus behind him to hold him in his saddle. By the time the two wounded men crossed over to the Ebenezer trail, Gabriel had gone limp. When they reached Ebenezer, he was dead. Lightner wept like a child, as did all the Salzburgers who saw their fallen hero. He even forgot to push his hair over his balding pate.

Pastor Boltzius let bygones be bygones and gave a eulogistic funeral oration praising this true Gideon.

"Our Gracious Lord is to be glorified for granting this erstwhile sinner to repent in time and crawl like a little worm into the wounds of Jesus." Gabriel was buried with due pomp and ceremony in the Jerusalem Church cemetery with the firing of twelve muskets.

"It 's strange," Rowner stammered to Lightner afterwards, "that I never noticed Gabriel's remarkable spiritual rebirth."

A searching party set out to recover Kumpan's remains. Because Boltzius would not allow the dog to be buried at his master's side in hallowed ground, Rowner and Leitner saw to it that Gabriel was buried right next to the fence, only an arm's length from his companion's unhallowed grave.

Margo reached Ebenezer a week later to put flowers on Gabriel's grave. She had sworn an oath to Gabriel that she would not travel alone, and it took her that long to find a fitting escort.

110

9

The Widow Bach

When word of Gabriel's death reached Margo, she did not swoon, as a well-bred widow should, but she did shed copious tears. She knew she would miss him terribly, miss those muscular arms around her. However, she also realized that they had been drifting apart for some time. He would never join the world she was now entering, he would never share her dream of the Gilded Coach.

Margo bit her lips and wondered what she would do now as a widow. She also reflected upon her marriage. This was never a real marriage because Gabriel was never a real husband. He was a lover, a serious and loyal but sporadic lover. The bond that held them together so firmly was mainly a mutual fulfillment of physical desire, as well as a pleasant fellowship.

I remember the hurt I felt, she reminisced, when I first noticed that he never came home during my monthly periods. He must have known my cycle. He was around to warm my bed only when it was convenient for him. In other words, he didn't come home for my company as much as for sex. I must admit that he never demanded sex, but possibly only because he never had to. Perhaps my love was an addiction. Maybe it wasn't love. Maybe it was just erotic desire. At any rate, I miss him intensely.

Margo remembered the verse by Richard Lovelace so often quoted by the older Mrs. Horton:

> I could not love thee, dear, so much,
> Loved I not honour more.

For Gabriel, "honor" meant glory. She had never entirely forgiven him for confronting the "Spaniard" man-to-man instead of shooting him from ambush, as Bichler assured her Gabriel could have done without any risk. Gabriel liked danger for its own sake. He was more of a warrior than a lover, a devotee of Mars rather than of Venus.

~

Margo resigned herself to her widowhood, enjoying the moral support of the older Mrs. Horton, who gave her some very elegant, even if passée, widow's weeds. With a bit of alteration they again looked stylish on Margo's slender yet voluptuous figure.

Mrs. Horton continued to cultivate and refine her little protégée. The older woman, a blue stocking in her day, supervised her reading from her own extensive library as well as from books borrowed from Mrs. Demere and, with much delay, from friends in Charleston.

The most influential of these books was Samuel Richardson's dreary and teary epistolary novel *Pamela*, which one of Mrs. Horton's London friends had sent to her posthaste as soon as it appeared. I cannot really be much concerned about Pamela's overwhelming concern for her virtue, Margo concluded. After all, I owed my own virginity on my wedding night to the Schneider women. Somehow Margo did not think of her previous marriage with Stout.

Margo was pleased that Mrs. Horton wished her to read Pamela's letters to her time after time, correcting all mispronunciations while shedding copious tears into her handkerchief.

"Have you read Henry Fielding's *Shamela?*" the younger Mrs. Horton asked Margo, pulling her aside and keeping her voice at a whisper.

"No, not yet," Margo replied, wondering why all the secrecy.

"It's a charming parody of *Pamela*, which I have just received and hidden."

"Why hidden?"

"It is not for anyone like my dear mother-in-law, who takes the original so seriously. She would simply die if she read it. The heroine, Shamela, is a shameless little hussy who manipulates men by pretending to be concerned about her virtue. Please be sure that the book never comes into Mother Horton's hands."

Although Margo had questioned the sentimentality in *Pamela*, she knew it was the very book from which to learn English. The vocabulary was simple because it was that of a teenage girl. In time Margo's English vocabulary broadened and her diction became flawless through the widow Horton's careful tutelage. She had even lost the harsh consonants and singsong lilt of her native dialect, and she had mastered the English *th*. She even referred to her former feline pet as Panther instead of Panzer.

Learning to read was the turning point in her life, even more significant than the disastrous voyage to America. Without leaving her chair she could now conjure up distant places and remote times and speak personally with great poets and thinkers. Until now, she thought, I was like a silkworm in its cocoon; now I have broken through, and the whole world has opened to me.

Margo read not only Milton, Bunyan, Defoe, Dryden, Richardson, and Fielding but also Cervantes, Rabelais, and other authors in English translation. The most disturbing book for Margo was Defoe's *Moll Flanders*, whose intriguing heroine was even more shameless than Shamela herself.

～

One evening the Hortons invited the Demeres to dinner. Hearing that Oglethorpe had just returned from a reconnaissance, they also sent him an invitation, which he accepted with pleasure. On such occasions Margo had usually entertained and fed the children and perhaps also helped serve the meal, but this time she was invited as a guest, another woman having been hired to do the serving. That meant she was the dinner partner of the famous hero, whom she so greatly admired. She had often curtsied to him on the street, and he had always doffed his tricorn and wished her a good day. Of course he did this to every lady, yet Margo felt that he was particularly cordial to her.

Margo had been well prepared for this occasion by the older Mrs. Horton's thorough training, and she felt very much at ease. She was not the least afraid that she might use the wrong fork or spoon. Even the well-born Oglethorpe included her in his conversation, asking for her opinion on this and that; and both of them radiated charm. The menu, in which Margo had played a major role, was excellent and the guest of honor in good spirits.

When the wine was passed, General Oglethorpe (still a colonel officially) proposed a toast to his Highland troops who had distinguished themselves so well at Bloody Marsh. All glasses emptied, Major Horton warned, "Be careful not to flick any wine in the General's face." Everyone laughed heartily but Margo, who did not understand the allusion. Seeing her bewilderment, Horton told the story of one of Oglethorpe's youthful deeds.

"When our guest of honor was a young officer just twenty years old."

"Just nineteen," Oglethorpe corrected him.

"When our honored guest was just nineteen, he was on the staff of Prince Eugene of Savoy during his campaign against the Turks. One night, while they were toasting their victory at Belgrade, a young German officer of princely rank, upon emptying his glass, flicked the remaining few drops into Oglethorpe's face. Standing up, the Englishman said very calmly, 'That's not the way we do it in England. We do it like this' and threw a full glass of wine into the other officer's face. When the prince jumped up and drew his sword, a senior officer said to him, 'Put away your sword, young man. You started it, and you deserved what you got.'"

The party continued jovially; but, soon after the nuts and peach brandy were served, the guest of honor made his excuses.

"It rained all day and I was unable to take any notes, so I must hurry home and write down all my observations before I forget what I've seen."

The general had hardly expressed his thanks and taken his leave before the young Mrs. Horton said, "I don't suppose Mrs. Hawkins will be lonesome tonight."

"Now don't be catty, Helen," her mother-in-law scolded.

"You know as well as I do where he is going."

"That's his right and his business," Major Horton protested. "The elderly Dr. Hawkins doesn't care. After all, he was not too proud to accept the highest civilian office on the island, even if it did all but banish him to the southern tip of the island."

Margo was rather bewildered by all this. Nobody had told her about Oglethorpe's secret love-life. She vaguely remembered hearing how Mrs. Hawkins made life unbearable for Charles Wesley when he disapproved of her morals, and she wondered whether Oglethorpe had been involved.

~

A week later Margo was watching Oglethorpe talking with a group of his Highlanders, in whose honor he was wearing kilts and plaid. Something seemed to be going wrong in their conversation. She called a greeting, and suddenly there was a loud explosion. One of the soldiers had fired point blank at Oglethorpe just as he turned to return Margo's greeting. The ball just missed him, the powder even scorched the queue of his wig.

Other Highlanders wrestled the man to the ground. The paymaster had not shown up, and the very drunk soldier could get no more credit at the canteen or borrow any money from his buddies. His addled brain put the blame on Oglethorpe.

~

As a Christian duty, Margo took on the care of Ensign Louis Delegal, a young South Carolina officer seriously wounded on shipboard just before the Battle of Bloody Marsh when Oglethorpe ordered all his ships to break through the Spanish blockade of Frederica.

"What happened to him?" Margo asked the silver-haired surgeon.

"A Spanish shell exploded on the deck, hurling a large fragment into his thigh. It was a jagged piece of metal which I removed with great difficulty, causing excruciating pain."

When Delegal's friends returned to Charleston after the victory, he was too weak to go with them; and they never really expected to see him again.

"The wound is both sore and sad," the surgeon reported the next time he saw Margo. "We have given up all hope of recovery. All I ask of you is to make the lieutenant's demise as painless as possible."

Margo tried to be cheerful, and she read poetry to her hero to distract him from his pain.

~

115

When not visiting her patient, Margo began taking part in the life of Frederica, which was quickly recovering from war and rumors of war. The most welcome addition was Frederica's newly-arrived German pastor, Johann Ulrich Driesler, who quickly endeared himself to everyone in the colony, both Dutch and English. Driesler was a true saint. One of the Scottish soldiers summed up the general opinion with the words, "That Dutch preacher lives like he preaches and he don't fare no better than the least of his parishioners." Driesler had not yet received a penny of the wages promised him, even though Oglethorpe had offered to pay the new clergyman from his own pocket if that proved necessary.

While everyone loved and admired the new minister, they did find him a bit too strict. Driesler regretted all the nice things that Horton said about the German congregation's good behavior, fearing that they might think they could achieve salvation by good works alone.

"A trust in one's own merits," he preached, "is but a snare of the devil. No amount of good behavior and good works can achieve salvation. One must be reborn in Jesus. One must recognize his own depravity and trust fully in the merits of our crucified Lord."

This worried Margo, who thought good works sufficient. Mrs. Horton noticed that her protégée usually looked depressed after returning from Driesler's sermons.

～

Driesler blamed the Indians' dreadful blasphemy on the British, who constantly took the name of the Lord in vain.

"But the British are not the only guilty ones," Margo objected. "The Indians' favorite oath here is 'God nimm my soul'. There is no way to explain the *nimm* other than that they have confounded 'God take my soul' with *Gott nimm meine Seele*. The German-speaking civilians around here outnumber the English-speaking ones, and doubtless some of them are blasphemous, at least when Driesler isn't around."

Driesler had arrived on the *McLane*, a vessel tightly packed with Highlanders, who had suffered dreadfully down in the fetid belly of the little ship. The *McLane* also brought a bevy of women recruited in London as wives for the soldiers.

"They are a questionable lot," the straight-laced pastor complained.

One female passenger had been keel-hauled for trying to kill her Highland husband, but even the involuntary swim behind the ship did not improve her behavior. Reputable or not, these "mermaids", as the puritanical clergyman called them, all found instant husbands. The single men on the outlying islands who arrived late had to remain bachelors for a while longer. About this time Oglethorpe requested the Trustees to send more brides for his soldiers and more German indentured laborers for his fort and fields.

Margo remembered the older Mrs. Horton's admonition not to corrupt her English by conversing with these new arrivals.

~

Driesler's all-too-short life at Frederica would have been even shorter if he had been standing, rather than sitting at his desk, one fateful afternoon. While he was preparing his next day's sermon, a musket ball came flying through his window and made a fist-sized hole in the tabby wall just above his head. It had been fired accidentally by an indentured servant, whose master had ordered him to clean and oil his weapon to keep it ready in case the Spaniards should attack again.

"Give him fifty lashes," the disciplinary Major Horton commanded.

"But it was just an accident," Driesler objected, "and no one got hurt." At his urging, Horton remitted the punishment. Margo was serving as interpreter on this occasion, her English now being entirely adequate.

Driesler was unintentionally lenient with the next offender, Carl Rudolf, "Prince of Wurttemberg", a strange character who claimed to be of royal blood. He looked the part. Delicate features, soft callous-free fingers, and perfect German diction with no trace of dialect.

According to Carl Rudolf's story, he had been kidnapped in London and sold as a slave to Oglethorpe, who had pressed him into military service. Driesler, himself a Wurttemberger, did not believe his tale or even recognize his dialect when the imposter came to him for help. To reassure himself, Driesler asked Margo to question the questionable prince.

"Where are you from?" Margo asked.

117

"Crailsheim," the self-styled prince answered after a brief hesitation. The answer could not have been more unfortunate for him, because Driesler was from Crailsheim.

"The surprising thing," the pastor avowed, "is that the documents the prince is carrying are excellently composed, well-penned, and provided with apparently authentic official seals."

One night Carl Rudolf was caught sleeping on the watch and was sentenced to run the gauntlet. Before having the sentence carried out, Major Horton discussed the matter with Driesler and mistakenly thought that the kindhearted parson was speaking on the culprit's behalf. The impostor was pardoned, yet his behavior did not improve. He continued taking advantage of his naive countrymen.

"The British government is sending out a warship for me to command," he confided to his listeners. "When it comes, I will take you all to Pennsylvania free of charge, and you will not have to finish your indentures."

~

Early one morning a bald and bearded messenger from Vernonburg sought out the widow Bach, as Margo had been called ever since Gabriel's death.

"What is it?" Margo asked.

"A message from Mrs. O'Connor," the courier answered.

"And who is Mrs. O'Connor?"

"The former widow Augusta Schneider," the out-of-breath courier explained. "She married her Irish servant and wants you to know she has a place for you to stay if you ever come to Vernonburg. She's sold her house in Savannah. O'Connor now speaks some German, better than he speaks English, even though Mrs. O'Connor is helping him learn both languages. He's done well with their farm, which was praised by Colonel Stephens himself just last week."

"How about her daughter Liesbeth?"

"She's married to her indentured servant, a chap named Murphy. They have a farm at Vernonburg, too; and she's expecting shortly."
"And how about John Stout?"

"He's managing a large plantation in South Carolina and has a farm of his own."

Margo was delighted to hear of the success of these three worthy people.

~

"Fire, fire!," Margo's former neighbor Alice Salton shouted one windy day. She had been frying mullet in opossum grease, when her pan caught on fire and the flames ignited her wall of dried palmetto branches. The fire then spread to the next house and raced down the street from house to house. The woman grabbed up her few possessions and fled, just in time, because the flames quickly reached the arsenal, which exploded with a mighty roar and hurled shot and shell far up into the sky. By the grace of God, no one was injured by the falling debris. The next day Margo saw two wagon loads of metal being picked up in front of her former house.

"Did you hear about Prieber?" Alice asked Margo later that week.

"No, what about him?"

"He was in the arsenal the whole time and didn't get killed," Alice answered.

Christian Gottlieb Prieber was a Saxon visionary who had come to America to organize the Noble Savages to defend themselves from European encroachment. Margo remembered Wiggins' remark about the do-gooder in the Georgia mountains, who wasn't going to get very far. The young Mrs. Horton, who had just joined the group, asked why Prieber was locked up in the arsenal. Alice proceeded with her account:

"Hearing that Prieber was stirring up the Cherokees in the Georgia mountains, the governor of South Carolina sent a delegation to arrest him, but the Cherokees wouldn't give up their guest."

"Then how did the British catch him?" Margo asked Alice.

"Capt. Richard Kent, the commanding officer at Augusta, bribed some Creeks to kidnap him on one of his diplomatic missions to the French or Spanish. His Negro servant was killed and he was brought to Frederica and confined in a cell next to the arsenal." The narrator, a humble woman, did not know that Prieber's cell had become a *salon* for the few intellec-

119

tual visitors at Frederica. They considered him a true *philosophe*, as people then called learned men who put more faith in reason than in religion.

On two occasions Gabriel had taken Margo with him when he visited Prieber to ask specific questions about the current relations between the Creeks and the Cherokees, and Margo said later,

"I'm surprised that he could understand my Swiss dialect so easily. He says he's never been in Switzerland."

"If he can understand Greek and Creek," Gabriel said, "I guess he can understand almost anything, even Schwyzer Duetsch." Actually, Prieber's doctoral dissertation had been written in Latin, not in Greek.

Alice continued, "When the arsenal exploded and everyone else fled in terror, Prieber remained sitting on his cot with perfect composure as the exploding shells and grenades fell around him."

Unfortunately, Prieber died a few months later of fever. His journal, in French, was either lost or perhaps purposely destroyed so that it would not disprove the accusation that he was a Jesuit.

$\sim$

"My pet aversion at Frederica," Driesler declared, "is not the incarcerated free-thinking Prieber but Thomas Bosomworth, the new Anglican minister. He's been sent to replace that seducer Norris, and that's no improvement."

Having crossed the ocean with Bosomworth on the *McLane*, Driesler knew him for a godless opportunist; and he particularly resented the fact that the English cleric never preached and held only occasional prayer services based on the *Book of Common Prayer*, while leaving all baptisms, marriages, and funerals to the overworked Lutheran minister and his broken English.

Driesler also noticed that the English preacher had an open eye for the young women of his parish. Bosomworth's attention was immediately drawn to Margo, who was now wearing widow's weeds altered to the latest style.

"Would you like to be my housekeeper?" Bosomworth asked benevolently.

"No, thank you very much, Sir. Mrs. Horton needs me." Margo remembered Elisabeth Penner's debacle, and she also remembered the double meaning of the word 'housekeeper'.

Driesler especially hated the task of marrying the lazy and avaricious British clergyman to the twice-widowed and very wealthy linguister, or interpreter, Mary Musgrove. Oglethorpe had called her down from her prosperous trading station on the Savannah for his talks with his Indian allies. Driesler was at last relieved of his burden when the Bosomworths moved back to her lucrative cowpen and trading house on the Savannah River, from which the ambitious cleric went on Sundays to preach in Savannah.

"How does Mary keep her store running now that those Scots have opened up their trading station?" Margo asked Driesler. "It's twenty miles upstream and much nearer the Indians."

"She keeps a display case full of worthless trinkets in front of the store between the two windows where the people in the store can't watch it. That means the Indians can steal at will. They are only human and want to get something for nothing, so they paddle the extra forty miles down to and back from Mary's store."

"But isn't that expensive for Mary?"

"Not really," Driesler answered. "She covers the loss by paying much less for the deerskins than the Scots do."

❧

Walking along the Frederica waterfront one morning, Margo saw a well-dressed young man hanging on the gallows.

"Who's that?" she asked a fat man pushing a wheelbarrow.

"He was the new surgeon. The son of very respectable parents in Dublin."

"What did he do?"

"He committed sodomy."

"And what's that?"

"It's a, well, it's a, it's something forbidden in the Old Testament," the embarrassed laborer replied. Margo's curiosity continued until Mrs. Horton delicately explained the situation.

❧

121

Some three weeks after Gabriel's death, Margo received an unexpected letter from James Habersham, formerly the manager of the Bethesda orphanage but now a prosperous merchant in Savannah.

Savannah, June 12, 1743

My dear Mrs. Bach,

Please accept my heartfelt condolences for your recent bereavement, which was a sad loss for all of us in Georgia.

Unbeknownst to you, your late husband has kept an account with me in your name, his monies being put out at eight percent interest. The balance is now £124.9.6 Sterling. You may withdraw the sum now if you so desire or else you may leave it out at interest. Please let me know your pleasure.

I have the Honour to be,
with great Respect, Madam,
Your most obedt. and humble Servt.
James Habersham

Margo was astounded. She had no idea that Gabriel had earned so much money, he seemed so utterly carefree and above money matters. She had often worried about what they would live on when he was cashiered, because an enlisted man's pension was even less than the pitiful pay he earned for risking his life. She remembered how abstemious he was, and how temperate, drinking mostly smallbeer rather than wine. Above all, he refrained from gambling, which was his comrades' chief amusement.

Margo also remembered that Gabriel was allowed to charge for delivering private mail and that he took many deer skins to Azuki to be tanned and sold. Margo did not know that Gabriel's thorough-bred stallion brought high stud fees and that he sometimes earned gratuities for bringing in lost cattle. He could also keep the unbranded cattle he found if no one laid claim to them for six months. Margo was especially touched that Gabriel had been so frugal just for her sake. She still felt a gnawing guilt at having questioned his fidelity.

~

Returning home one afternoon from the invalided lieutenant's bedside, Margo stopped to watch some children crabbing at the end of a little wooden pier jutting out into the river just below the fort. Boys and girls of all ages were laughing and shouting whenever one of them pulled up a crab.

"I gotta bite," a little boy called gleefully, slowly pulling up his line. In addition to the sinker and piece of meat, there was a gluttonous and unsuspecting crab tearing at the bait.

"Caroline, bring the net," he called. The oldest girl scooped up the crab with a net shaped like a butterfly net but much sturdier. By now they had a bushel basket brimming with crabs.

Margo stood watching the happy children until suddenly she heard a many-voiced scream. One of the smaller girls had lost her balance and fallen into the strong ebb current. Stifling her own scream, Margo rushed headlong to the end of the pier, kicked off her shoes, and dropped her heavy skirt before jumping into the river. By then the current had carried the struggling child at least fifty feet from the pier, but Margo caught up with her just in time to reach down and pull her to the surface. Holding the distraught girl's head above water, Margo calmed and comforted her until she gained control of herself and could breathe again.

"Just hang on to me," Margo ordered. She then turned around slowly until the child was in back of her and clinging to her shoulders. Margo headed for land with her best breast stroke and frog kick. She did not try to return to the dock, rather she let the current carry her downstream while she steadily neared the shore, which she finally reached some hundreds of yards below the dock. As she helped the child ashore, she was met by the other children and scores of excited spectators, one of whom gave her a cloth to wear as a skirt. Later in the day Margo was congratulated by General Oglethorpe himself.

"A job well done!" the General said.

In her heart Margo gave the credit for her deed to Gabriel, who had made her learn to swim.

123

10

Lieutenant Delegal

One invigorating day, after visiting the wounded lieutenant Delegal, Margo curtsied on the street to Mrs. Demere, who asked, "Have you heard about the two Spanish boys?"

"No, tell me."

"They were captured by Indians after the Battle of Bloody Marsh and sold to Mary Musgrove, who sent them to labor as slaves at her cowpen on the Savannah River."

"But I thought slavery was forbidden in Georgia."

"It's forbidden for white people," Mrs. Demere continued, "but the Indians have their own laws, and slavery has always been their custom. The two boys tried to escape. They stole a rowboat and went down the river, passing Savannah unseen, probably at night. They were first spotted by the lighthouse guard at Tybee, who didn't have the means to chase them. Somehow the boys rounded the point and went out into the ocean and turned south for Florida."

"Did they have a sail?" Margo showed great concern.

"No, just oars. They went ashore on Ossabaw to find food, and there they were caught by an Indian hunting party that happened to be on the island. As you probably know, Ossabaw is one of the islands that Tomochichi retained when he gave land to the English. The Indians could have burned them to death for escaping, but they preferred to demand a reward from Mary Musgrove. Apparently, all the Indians in Georgia had been informed of their escape."

"And what became of them then?" Margo asked with real feeling.

"The Indians took 'em to the mainland in their canoes and made them walk all the way back to Mary's cowpen carrying their own and all the Indians' equipment. Indian braves are much too noble to carry anything. They whipped the lads on their bare legs all the way back."

124

"Do you know whether the boys are still alive?" Margo could visualize the boys' bloody legs. She remembered the red stripes on a young sailor boy who had talked back to a superior.

"I suppose they're still alive, if they survived their punishment," Mrs. Demere answered. "Sometimes runaways have their feet partially amputated so they can't run away again."

Margo worried all night about the fate of the two renegades. The next morning she wrote a letter to Constable Bichler asking him to go to Mary's cowpen and redeem the boys at any cost and send them down to her.

Three weeks later the boys arrived at Frederica, and Margo sent Bichler the redemption money as well as a gratuity for his services. After finding a room for the half-starved youngsters and fattening them up and clothing them, she sent them back to Saint Augustine on a coastal trading boat. Although England and Spain were still at war, New England mariners did not scruple to trade with St. Augustine, where they received Mexican gold coins for their merchandize. Margo was not responsible for the two captives, yet she could not help wondering whether they may have been two of the four prisoners taken by Gabriel after Bloody Marsh.

It was the first time Margo had touched her legacy. She was astonished that one of the renegades was fair haired, almost blond. She had always thought that all Spaniards were swarthy, like Dr. Mazzique and "the Spaniard".

❧

Margo noticed that Betsy was in foal. "Betsy, how could you do such a thing?"

Betsy whinnied an unintelligible excuse.

"You know why we kept you and Pegasus in separate stalls and tethered you apart. Surely you were not unfaithful."

When the filly was born, there was no more question of infidelity. Unable to maintain two horses, Margo offered the filly for sale. There were many bidders. Margo did not choose the highest bidder. She chose the kindest one.

While Margo enjoyed walking through the town in her black finery and receiving the curtsies of the women folk and the bows of the common men, she spent most of her time with the wounded lieutenant. She wished to repay the kindness shown her by Stout and to be a strong pillar of support for the young invalid. A naval orderly performed the most intimate services, while Margo quickly assumed all other tasks. She saw to it that the patient's bedclothes were changed regularly, that his nightgown was clean, his boyish face close shaven, and his food prompt and edible. The doctor, who came daily, was astonished that his patient was still alive and even appeared to be recovering.

Margo noticed that the lieutenant's eyes were identical to her own, sky blue and shaded by thick black lashes. In fact the two looked like brother and sister, and even their pronunciation was similar, his influenced by study in England and hers learned from the very cultivated English widow Horton, the descendant of a long line of Cambridge professors. Margo had not yet seen Louis stand; but she estimated that he was more than half a head taller than she, as an older brother should be.

"I am amazed," the patient mentioned during one of Margo's visits, "that a great warrior like Gabriel was fond enough of poetic inspiration to name his horse Pegasus. As you know, Pegasus represented poetic inspiration. He never had to pull a cart or a plow, or even carry a man. He just soared through the air on his great white wings. Perhaps that's why poets so often starve in garrets."

"But at least they are happy while they are starving," Margo said, pulling up his blanket.

"To get back to the subject," the young invalid resumed, "it was a shame Gabriel had to die so young. He had a brilliant future before him."

"He never thought of the future," Margo countered. "He lived entirely in the present. His ruling passions were to obey and give commands and do his duty. He really had no ambition, he was completely satisfied as long as life was exciting and dangerous. He reached his ultimate goal the day he was promoted to sergeant. He had no desire to be an officer, he wasn't even jealous of Milledge for being a captain with so much less

126

experience than he had. He would surely have preferred to die in battle in the prime of youth rather than end up toothless and with aching bones in some old soldiers home."

⁓

The conversation, always lively, jumped back and forth. Margo related how she had called up the pigs when she yodeled at Fort Argyle.

"It's lucky you weren't in France when you yodeled."

"Why's that?"

"Because it's a serious offence to yodel in France."

"How so?"

"Whenever the Swiss Guards and other Swiss mercenaries hear a yodel, they begin deserting." Lewis attempted a yodel, but not very successfully. "It is said that the Swiss guards are afflicted by *heimweh*, as you call homesickness."

Margo, who was arranging some flowers in a vase, changed the subject,

"How do we discover the names of all these new plants and animals in Georgia?"

"We don't discover them. We invent and assign them." Reaching to his bedside Bible, Louis, or Lewis as he called himself, thumbed through Genesis and said, "The Good Book explains it this way. After God made all the animals and birds, He `brought them unto Adam to see what he would call them. And whatsoever Adam called every living creature, that was the name thereof.' The trouble is that Adam never came to Georgia. And he didn't name any plants, so we have to do it"

"And how do we do it?" Margo asked, pushing back an unruly wisp of hair.

"We just name the plants as we wish," Lewis answered. "When the English came here they had no names for many of the local animals and plants. Usually they gave plants and animals the names of the most similar ones back home, but often incorrectly. For example, the robin redbreast here is entirely unlike the robin in Europe, and what we call a trout here is not a trout, but a bass. There were no elks in England, as there were in Sweden. When the first Englishman saw one in America and asked an Indian what it was, the Indian said ' moose'. That's how we got such words as opossum, raccoon, and skunk."

"But who decides which Indian name will be used," Margo queried. "I hear that every tribe in Georgia has its own language."

"That's decided by the Royal Society in London. If you wish to name a bird, animal, serpent, plant, or tree that has not been named, all you have to do is send it, or a drawing of it and a good description, to Dr. Hans Sloane of the Society, and he will make the name you give it official for the whole world if it's not yet recorded. But it's recorded in its Latin form."

"Why in Latin?" Margo asked. "I thought Latin was a dead language."

"Latin's not dead, it grows every time we identify a new bird, animal, or fish. It's the international language of science." Picking up a little white flower from the bouquet Margo had brought, Lewis continued,

"I think I should send this little daisy-like flower to the Royal Society and have them name it *chrysanthemum margonensis*, because it is as white as your throat. Some twenty years ago there was an English naturalist roaming around Georgia who gave names to literally hundreds of plants and animals and fish. His name was Mark Catesby."

"He must be the person Catesby's Swamp was named for," Margo suggested, fondling Lewis' daisy. "Do you think I could name something, too?"

"Certainly."

"There's an ugly little creature at Fort Argyle. Captain Milledge says it's found only on the banks of the Ogeechee, and nowhere else in the world. It's black, about as long as my index finger, and much thicker. It ought to be a grasshopper, but it can't hop. It just trudges along on the ground."

"And what do you wish to name it?" Lewis asked.

"How about *insectus Bosomworthensis?* I think the name would be most suitable."

"I shall write to Hans at once."

∾

"Who was Gustavus Adolphus?" Margo asked one day, abruptly changing the subject after a long conversation.

"A Swedish King who helped the Protestants in the Thirty Years War. And why do you ask?"

"Oh, I don't know. I was just wondering. And when was the Thirty Years War?"

"From 1618 to the Treaty of Westphalia in 1648."

Lewis was curious as to why Margo so often changed the subject and why she so often asked who someone or what something was. Children often ask for identities and then dismiss them from mind, having asked just to hear themselves talk. Lewis doubted that this was Margo's purpose, but one afternoon he put her to the test.

"Who was Pegasus?"

"A mythological horse representing poetic inspiration."

"Who was Gustavus Adolphus?"

"A king of Sweden who helped the Protestants during the Thirty Years war."

"And how long did the Thirty Years War last?"

"Thirty Years, from 1618 till the Treaty of Westphalia in 1648."

"And who is Hans Sloane?"

"An English naturalist who is registering all species of flora and fauna. If you send him a specimen and a description of its habitat, he will give it whatever name you choose. But in Latin."

"And what are flora and fauna?"

"Plants and living creatures. Is there anything else you would like to know?"

Lewis decided then and there that Margo was really driven by intellectual, not idle, curiosity. After that he took still keener pleasure in answering her many questions, and he even began asking her questions of which he did not know the answers. The Widow Horton's reading courses were standing Margo in good stead.

~

Margo discovered that Lewis was familiar with most of the poems Mrs. Horton had selected for her and knew many of them by heart. Despite his modesty, she soon learned that he had studied at Eton and Oxford and had devoted more time to the classics and current literature than to the theology his parents wished him to study.

With the gradual return of his strength, Lewis began taking turns in the poetry reading. Margo was touched by the tender feelings expressed by his voice, which were a far-cry from Gabriel's military commands. The intellectual curiosity they shared made it clear that Margo and Lewis were soul mates.

Margo felt she was playing the role of the crow that wore borrowed feathers. She feared that Lewis would be disappointed when the false feathers came off, as they surely would in time. To free him of any delusions, she told him the truth about her childhood on the alpine slopes, her tiring work of herding the goats and cattle, her lack of schooling, and the loss of the farm.

"I was even a *wilderer* at age thirteen."

"What's that?"

"In most of Germany that means a poacher, but at home it means a person who scrambles around among the rocks to cut and gather the grass the cows can't reach. It's backbreaking work and very dangerous. Two girls in our village fell to their deaths in three years. I had a nasty fall myself," Margo said, raising her skirt and showing a scar near her knee. Lewis admired the leg, despite the scar. Because Margo had been wearing the widow Horton's weeds with their long skirts, he had never seen her above her ankles.

"The few sacks of hay harvested by a *wilderer* sometimes determine whether or not a cow will survive the winter in case of a late spring."

"Why did you have to emigrate just because you lost your farm?" Lewis asked. "Couldn't you move to town and find jobs?"

"No chance. For every job there were fifty hungry applicants, each eager to undersell all the others. Besides that, bankruptcy is a disgrace. Even one's closest kinsmen turn their backs, attributing the failure to incompetence or shiftlessness, or else to a punishment of God."

"Couldn't a bankrupt man go somewhere else?"

"Not in Switzerland. He would have no right of domicile. A man

130

without kin or roots is a vagabond and will soon slip down into the *unehrliche Leute*, the `dishonorable people'."

"Who are they?" Lewis asked.

"They are the vagabonds, tramps, drunks, and other people who live on the fringes of society. They usually hang out together in abandoned shacks or caves. They can find only "dishonorable" and dirty jobs such as working for charcoal burners, kettle burnishers, and skinners. They have no legal rights and can't even be buried in holy ground. I suppose in time they will all come to America."

Margo also related the death of all her family on the disastrous voyage, as well as her two marriages. Lewis was not fazed, and he often insisted,

"I'm not concerned with the past but only with the future. If you survived such a past, you'll have no difficulty with the future."

"I hope you're right, but I'm not so sure."

~

"Now that you've told me your past," Lewis said, "I should tell you of my great inner conflict. I'm to be a minister of the gospel, yet I don't believe much of the Bible. I had to learn Greek in order to read the New Testament, but I spent much more time reading the Greek classics, and I preferred Plato and Aristotle to the Church Fathers. I feel so hypocritical preaching about the Holy Ghost, the Trinity, and the Virgin Birth when I don't really believe in them."

"Then why are you going to be a preacher?" Margo asked.

"Because I think Christ's message, as expressed in the beatitudes, is better than what our pagan ancestors believed in."

Lewis apologized for his own humdrum life as pupil and student and also for his one month's inconspicuous naval service with a rank owed to his family's influence rather than to his own merits. Margo gradually realized that Lewis felt he just wasn't good enough for her. Although slightly older than she, he was far less experienced; and his reticence gave her a sense of self-esteem she had never known before.

"Your life would really make a dramatic story," Lewis said. "In his *Poetics* Aristotle states that a hero has to pass from misfortune to happiness or from happiness to misfortune. You certainly had your share of misfortune, and now you have passed to happiness, haven't you?"

"But you said Aristotle also ruled that a drama must have a conflict. I never really had a conflict, just adversities. To be sure, I suffered 'the slings and arrows of outrageous fortune,' but I was always passive. Captain Wadham and the *Europa* may have struggled against the sea, but I took no part in the conflict, I was barely alive and tied to my bunk. The only great conflict in my life was competing with Azuki for Gabriel's love, and that fight was entirely in my mind."

～

One sunny morning the recuperating lieutenant said, "Margo, I love you just as you are. I hope you will never change but stay the same for ever. However, if we are to marry and live in South Carolina, we will have to live as the Carolinians do, however stupid that may be."

Margo was taken aback. There had been no talk of love or marriage.

Lewis continued, "South Carolinians live in a never-never world of chivalry. Every planter there has illustrious ancestors, mostly bogus, because London genealogists can furnish anyone with an ancient line for five pounds Sterling. My brother-in-law Edward Pinckney, although otherwise intelligent, firmly believes that our family fought on both sides at the Battle of Hastings; but I know for a fact that one of our grandfathers, an alleged 'second son'. . ."

"What's a 'second son?'" Margo asked.

"That's a son who has no inheritance. Also a fancy word for an indentured servant. One of our grandparents was actually a simple indentured servant of humble origins who got rich in Bermuda and sent his sons off for a good education in England. It was also rumored that another of our forebears always wore a right hand glove. If that's so, he must have been hiding the brand burned on the hands of deported criminals to keep them from returning to England.

"Good for him!"

"In time we'll have to concoct a family tree for you going back to Charlemagne, because as of now you are a Huguenot."

"But I can't speak French," Margo objected.

"Nor can anyone in our family," Lewis admitted. "Grandfather Delegal was the only Huguenot in our family, and he spoke only English because his parents had lived so long in England and his wife spoke only English. You are now the widow Bacques. If we retained the spelling Bach, it would be pronounced Batch or Back. I doubt that one out of fifty Carolina planters has heard of Johann Sebastian."

"I never did either, until you mentioned him."

"Also, your late and only husband was *Captain* Bacques, who died gloriously in His Majesty's service. A friend of mine in the Admiralty has promised to see that the rank and spelling are corrected in our military records."

To show her appreciation, Margo gave Lewis a grateful kiss. To her surprise, the kiss became more than a token of gratitude; and she had to use will power to terminate it within the limits of propriety.

Margo told Lewis about her Gilded Coach dream.

"I guess you've picked the wrong husband," Lewis confessed. "Country Parsons don't usually ride around in gilded coaches, certainly not with coachman and postilion. We will be lucky to have a buggy."

"Oh, I can do without a real gilded coach if I can just keep my dream of *the* Gilded Coach." Patting his hand, she added, "As long as I have you."

～

Wishing to make the widow Bacques' transition to South Carolina society as painless as possible, Lewis asked his dearly beloved older sister Frances Pinckney to invite Margo to visit her at Port Royal, the little seaport just north of Savannah. Col. Edward Pinckney was away much of the time on military affairs or else supervising his rice plantation on the Santee, where he was building a magnificent mansion in Palladian style.

"I shall be delighted," Frances answered Lewis by return mail, "to have the company of my future sister-in-law while you are being medically discharged from the service and are studying in Charleston." Lewis had to take some more theological instruction from Commissary Alexander Garden, the Bishop of London's representative in Charleston.

"Just where is Charleston, precisely?" Margo asked.

"About a hundred miles north of Savannah, where the Ashley and Cooper Rivers join to form the Atlantic Ocean. Do you know how the Charlestonians are like the Chinese?" Lewis asked.

"No. Why?"

"Because they eat rice and worship their ancestors."

～

Margo traveled north from Frederica on Habersham's *Savannah Sloop*.

"How did Habersham come by such a big boat?" she asked the weather-beaten skipper.

"It used to belong to the Bethesda Orphanage," the mariner replied, emptying his pipe. "While building the orphanage Whitefield and his business manager, Habersham, found it advisable to own their own boat so as to buy their building materials in Philadelphia or Charleston, much cheaper than from the Savannah merchants. Once the building was completed, the orphanage no longer needed the sloop, so Habersham bought it for the mercantile business he recently started with Francis Harris."

"Is Harris the Englishman in Savannah who speaks such good German?" Margo asked.

"Yes," the old salt answered, "he's why Habersham gets most of the Salzburger and Dutch business."

～

Margo boarded the sloop at Frederica. When it stopped off at Darien for more cargo, she recognized some of her Highland friends who had fought so well at Bloody Marsh.

"Are the other Highlanders going to learn English, too?" Margo asked.

"Why should they?" one of the Scots queried. "Gaelic is all they need here at Darien since we have a pastor, the Reverend John McLeod, who preaches in Gaelic. And we have a commanding officer, Lt. George Gordon, who gives his orders in that language." It was ironic that Gaelic speaking soldiers from Scotland, Ireland, and Wales were helping spread the English language to all corners of the world.

With Frederica well fortified, the Highlanders' fort, Fort King George, was more or less abandoned. Only a few of the garrison were standing guard in their plaids and carrying their claymores and targets, their swords and shields. The others were busy felling trees and raising crops, if not playing their bagpipes or throwing logs. At Darien they found no stones to throw.

The winds being favorable, the sloop took the ocean route from Darien to Savannah to avoid the tedious meanderings of the inland waterway. That meant that Margo did not get to see the gallows at Hell's Gate, where, it was said, Shannon's bones were still hanging. On the way, Margo amused herself by feeding the sea gulls, either throwing bread up in the air to make them catch it or holding it up and making them take it from her fingers. She was not afraid of the birds' sharp beaks. They are like the harpies, she thought, remembering Lewis' account of those fabulous creatures. The playful dolphins also entertained her on her long voyage.

Upon reaching Savannah, Margo found the city in turmoil. Rangers and other mounted and uniformed men were milling around; and the German and German-Swiss militia troops from Hamstead, Acton, and Vernonburg and the French-speaking unit from Highgate had been called up. The handful of Moravians still in Savannah were about the only men not under arms.

"What's happening?" Margo asked a heavily armed stranger.

"Bosomworth and his wife Mary Musgrove are coming to town, and this is the welcoming committee."

"But why so many armed men?"

"Colonel Stephens was expecting just the two of them, but last night Noble Jones' son, Noble Wimberly, reported that they were bringing an escort of two hundred armed braves."

Before the speaker could continue, Mrs. O'Connor, the former widow Schneider, recognized Margo and embraced her warmly.

"When Patrick was mustered, I came to town with him to see what was happening. People say the Bosomworths are coming to town to claim

Ossabaw, Saint Catherine's, and Sapelo, three coastal islands."

"On what grounds?"

"When Tomochichi gave the Englishmen the land along the Savannah and along the Atlantic coast, the Indians kept those three islands as hunting grounds. With nice gifts and plenty of rum, Mary Musgrove got the Creek chiefs to call her their Empress and to let her claim the islands as her personal property. Obviously, Bosomworth is behind all this. He probably also suggested that they bring a large armed force to scare Colonel Stephens." Margo saw the venerable Secretary in uniform, bearing a sword.

A messenger galloped in to announce that the Bosomworths and their retainers were approaching the city, and Captain Jones called the cavalry to order and placed them in a double column at the Ebenezer Gate as a guard of honor for the guests. Lightner's and Rowner's dragoons were right behind them. Capt. Pierre Rudolf Morel lined up his French and German militia, all well armed, behind them.

Shortly, the Imperial retinue arrived, Bosomworth in his clerical robes and Mary in all the finery and ornamentation appropriate to her royal condition. Seeing the well-armed reception committee, the Indians concealed the sawed-off muskets that some were carrying under their blankets.

Far from being intimidated, Colonel Stephens and the members of the Council did not commit themselves regarding the islands but said they would have to consult the authorities in London first. Furnishing the Indians with abundant food and drink, the leading citizens kept them under surveillance until they staggered out of town the next day. The negotiations concerning the islands dragged on for years.

11

A Lady of Fashion

When Frances Pinckney met Margo at the Port Royal dock, she showed unfeigned enthusiasm.

"I am so happy to meet you after all my brother has written about you. And I'm so proud that my brother and your late husband helped turn back the Spaniards. As you know, it's been just forty years since the Spaniards and their Indians destroyed Port Royal and massacred all the inhabitants. They might have done it again this time if it weren't for men like Lewis and Gabriel."

Margo was barely able to insert an "I'm so happy to meet you . . ."

"What a shame you lost all your lovely wardrobe when those nasty Spaniards attacked. But it doesn't really matter, because we can go to Charleston and replace everything. Charleston is quite a metropolis."

Margo was glad she still had a hundred and two pounds credit with Habersham, who had business connections in Charleston.

～

The Pinckney residence in Port Royal was of brick, stately enough to house an English lord. It was built soon after the disastrous Yemassee War, in which all the houses, then mostly of wood, had been torched. The house stood at the water's edge and afforded a splendid view of the harbor, one of America's finest.

But even more welcomed than the architecture and the view was the mosquito net that surrounded Margo's entire four-poster bed. She had never seen such a luxury, even Mrs. Horton did not have one. She wondered how many years and hands it took to tie all those tiny knots.

The first gift Margo received from Frances was a lady's maid named Patience, a black but comely girl of seventeen, already an expert at lacing corsets, arranging coiffures, and performing other indispensable services.

"Why does Patience speak such good English?" Margo asked her future sister-in-law. "She speaks better than most whites in Savannah."

"Her family have been our domestic servants for nearly a century, long before our people brought them here from Barbados," Margo replied. "Her parents, Isaiah and Debra, speak just as well."

Shortly after praising Patience's good speech, Margo happened to overhear her talking with one of the field hands. They were speaking a gibberish of which Margo could not understand a single word.

"What language was Patience just speaking?"

"That's Gullah," Frances answered.

"Gullah?"

"It's the slaves' *lingua franca*. They came from a thousand miles of African coastline and have no language in common but English, which they seldom hear spoken by a white man. The makeshift language had already taken shape back in Barbados and was brought to Charleston by the first slaves who came here. All the Africans who've arrived since then have had to learn it."

"Why did you talk that way with Jupiter?" Margo asked her maid the next day.

"If I had talked as you do," the maid answered, "he would not have understood me. Besides that, I would have sounded too stuck up."

~

Margo soon learned that it was unladylike to do any kind of work, except perhaps embroidery and needle point. For home consumption or gifts to dear friends. Never for sale.

"Why can't I do my own work?" she asked Frances.

"It would be unbecoming. Also, it would offend the servants, who would think you weren't satisfied with what they did. It would also disgrace them in the eyes of the other blacks if their masters were seen working."

This ran counter to Margo's Swiss work ethic. Although her family had always been very poor, they were respected because they all worked so hard. Her father frequently quoted the maxim "Work makes life sweet."

Whenever Margo undressed herself, which was seldom since Patience insisted upon performing this chore, she learned to leave her clothes on chairs or on the floor and let Patience hang them up. Less than five years ago I was a servant, Margo mused. Now I *have* a servant. Unlike me, she will always be a servant. Can a leopard change his spots, or an Ethiopian his skin?

To occupy her time now that she was forbidden to work, Margo spent long hours at Frances' piano exercising her fingers and studying the notes. In a short while she could adequately render pieces by Purcell, Handel, and other recent composers. She also played the accompaniment to the games played by Frances' children.

∿

Frances' husband, Col. Edward Pinckney, finally came home for a short vacation after long talks with the Overhill Cherokees in Tennessee. All the neighbors invited the Pinckneys, including Lt. Delegal and his fiancée, to parties given to hear the latest on Indian affairs. Although the guests preferred to hear about the Indians, Pinckney was more concerned at the moment about a heresy that was spreading among the German Swiss some hundred miles from Charleston.

"A wild group the Swiss are," the aristocratic-looking Pinckney asserted, "with a few exceptions like our painter Jeremiah Theus and John Tobler, the mathematician and almanac maker at New Windsor. It's incredible how stupid most of them are."

It's lucky I'm a Huguenot now, Margo decided, and no longer a German Swiss.

Pinckney continued his story. "A farmer named Jacob Weber began holding Bible classes for his countrymen. Unfortunately, his audience so deified him that he became convinced he was God the Father. He thereupon appointed his friend Schmidt Peter to be God the Son, and an elderly black preacher joined them as the Holy Ghost."

"How long did the sect last?" Frances asked her husband.

"Too long," the colonel answered. "Christian Theus, the Swiss Reformed minister for the area and the brother of our painter friend Jeremiah Theus, came upon one of their meetings accidentally. When God the Son asked him whether he believed in their God the Father, the old man had the temerity to deny that Weber was God. Seeing the

139

congregation's anger, the minister broke and ran, with the congregation in hot pursuit. He reached the river in time to jump into a bateau, and the Negro boatman pushed off just as the murderous pack arrived."

"Did Theus get satisfaction?" Frances asked.

"God saw to that," Edward assured her. "God the Father and God the Son soon tired of the way the Holy Spirit was performing his duties, so they had a deep grave dug, threw the black man into it, and covered him with mattresses. Then the whole congregation marched across them until the victim was smothered."

"And what happened to the rest of the Trinity?"

"God the Father had God the Son chained to a tree, and the congregation competed in beating him to death with their fists."

"And God the Father?"

"The authorities in Charleston sent John Stout, the Orangeburg deputy sheriff, to arrest him, and he will be hanged next week for murder, not for heresy. All faiths are legal now in South Carolina."

Margo flinched at the name Stout. She was reassured, however, that he would never mention their short and illegal union. She trusted he could keep a secret as well as she, and her faith was strengthened when Pinckney continued:

"Stout's a good man. I've been trying to employ him for over a year, offering him much better terms than he has now, but he won't accept them."

"Why not?" Margo asked.

"Says he can't quit his mistress, a widow with two children, because she nursed him back to health when he arrived at Orangeburg almost sick to death. These Dutchmen really have an excessive sense of loyalty."

Margo felt sure she had heard the name Jacob Weber before. All at once she recalled he was one of the lucky few on the *Europa* who had not taken sick on the voyage and had continued the journey to South Carolina with Riemensperger.

≈

By now Margo's black mourning dresses were in excellent taste and her hair beautifully coiffured by Patience. Before she and Lewis set out for a reception at Hampton Hall, a magnificent Georgian-style mansion, Frances warned Margo,

"Tonight you are going to see the portrait of a gorgeous young woman, really still a child. The London painter did a remarkable job of capturing both her physical and her spiritual beauty. But please don't ask about her, because it brings up tragic memories."

"What happened to her?"

"Miss Ellen disappeared on the morning of her wedding. No one thought she had eloped like the Fenwick girl, for she and her groom were madly in love and their parents favored the union. Because it was to be a magnificent affair, kinsmen came from far away, bringing their children and grandchildren with them for the event.

"To entertain the children in the morning, Miss Ellen organized a game of hide and seek. When it was her turn to hide, the children could not find her even though they sought out all rooms, wardrobes, the attic, basement, and even the labyrinth in the garden. When they could not find her, their parents helped, but still no Miss Ellen. All the guests and all the slaves searched the entire plantation and even dragged the canals, but without any luck."

"What had happened to her?" Margo asked with more concern than curiosity.

"She had sneaked up to the attic and hidden in a trunk, in which she was found three years later."

~

The first time Frances and Margo went riding together, Frances was appalled that Margo wore no gloves.

"But it will make your hands so rough!"

Margo realized that riding gloveless was not the only reason her hands were rough. They are honest hands. They never shirked hard manual labor on our farm, and I carried wood and water for the Schneiders. I helped Stout with his hoeing, I milked the cows and did other chores at the Ebenezer orphanage. I even cultivated my garden at Fort Argyle. I still remember how my father used to recite that old Swiss proverb: "The hand that wields the hoe on Saturday can best caress on Sunday."

141

When the two young women returned home, Frances gave Margo a pair of riding gloves and a bottle of hand lotion, which Margo promised to use three times a day.

"You really should ride sidesaddle," Frances admonished. "Straddling a horse is too unladylike for a Delegal."

"But straddling is much safer."

"Then don't ride so fast, and don't jump."

Because Margo was going to marry her younger brother, Frances had the God-given right to treat her as a younger sister, and Margo had to give in. She also had to carry, or have a slave carry, a parasol to protect her face from the sun and keep it as pale as the faces of the other well-born ladies. Margo suspected that the wan faces around her resulted less from good birth than from malaria. She, too, had caught malaria in Savannah, but it afflicted her only a few days each spring and each fall.

$\sim$

Frances had provided her sister-in-law with a gentle little mare suitable for a lady, since Margo had left Betsy behind with Mrs. Horton. To assert herself, Margo wrote to Constable Bichler to please send her Pegasus, who had been earning his keep at Ebenezer as a stud horse. Two weeks later Bichler arrived with the white stallion. For riding back to Ebenezer, he had brought the horse he and Gabriel had taken from the "Spaniard." Margo wished to mount Pegasus at once but remembered it was unladylike to ride astride. Fortunately, her sidesaddle could be stretched to fit the sixteen-hand steed, and she learned to mount in a ladylike fashion from a mounting block.

Bichler looked much older than Margo remembered him. Sensing at once that something was wrong, Margo asked, "What's the matter, Mr. Bichler?"

"I've just been swindled and reduced to poverty and crushing debts by a confidence man named Curtius. Curtius, or Kurtz as he should be called because he's not a clergyman. He visited Ebenezer and proposed a big lumber deal. The Salzburgers were to supply him with beams, boards, shingles, and barrel staves in return for trade goods from Curtius' wealthy merchant uncle in New York."

"Was there really a rich uncle?"

"No, there wasn't; but Curtius was such a pious man while at Ebenezer and he attended all religious observances so zealously and prayed with such fervor that Boltzius and all of us were entirely taken in. I went with him to Charleston and signed several notes, which I could not read, in my and Pastor Boltzius' names."

"And what happened then?" Margo asked.

"The Salzburgers provided the promised timber and woodwork, all of which was freighted directly to Charleston to be forwarded to New York on a larger vessel. Hearing no more from the entrepreneur, I returned to Charleston and discovered that Curtius had sold all the lumber and wood-work for cash to a merchant, who had already shipped it to the West Indies. Speaking little English and knowing nothing about law or business, I could not cope with Curtius, who had a glib answer for every complaint."

Feeling sorry for the gullible constable, Margo decided to look into the matter during her impending journey to Charleston to buy her trous-seau.

～

On their way to Charleston, Frances and Margo stopped off to visit Lewis' kinsmen at Fenwick Hall on John's Island near Charleston. Fenwick Hall was a large Georgian-style brick residence, as elegant as any house Margo had ever seen in Switzerland. It was surrounded by well-groomed gardens, gardens laid out in grand style by an expert from London.

"That's the finest house I've yet seen in South Carolina," Margo exclaimed.

"Not nearly so grand," Frances boasted, "as the mansion my hus-band is building on the Santee."

Margo refrained from asking the Fenwicks whether the story of John Fenwick's runaway daughter was true. She thought it might well be true, judging by their obsession with their ancestry and that of their horses. Lewis had once said that if the Fenwicks wished to explain the origin of Pegasus, they would have said "he was by Poseidon out of Medura." Natu-rally, the equine generations, being shorter, went back farther than those of the Fenwicks.

Soon after leaving the mansion, Lewis asked Margo, "Did you ever hear about their ancestor Sir John Fenwick?"

"No, never did."

"The story is that Parliament was worried because he was running around calling on important people, apparently fomenting a revolution. Unable to get any evidence, Parliament passed a bill of attainder against him, making it possible to behead him without a trial. His three sons died soon after the beheading. According to family legend, after each funeral their mother dug them up, very much alive, and smuggled them to America. The family here is supposed to descend from one of the sons, but there is no proof.

~

Upon reaching Charleston, Margo asked one of Frances' distinguished cousins, a lawyer named Hopton, to investigate the Curtius deal. This he did immediately; and, proving fraud, he took out an injunction to stop all Curtius' business activities and to end his credit. Before the swindler could be apprehended, he fled to New York. Much of the Salzburgers' investment was recovered. Only Bichler had signed a personal note.

Having visited Charleston several times, Boltzius told Margo the fine ladies in Charleston held black masks over their faces when they went out on the unpaved streets to protect them from the dust and sand. He was right. One of the first things Margo saw in Charleston was ladies, either on foot or in open carriages, peering through black masks and making the town look like a masked ball.

While Frances and Margo were in Charleston, Colonel Pinckney insisted they use his coach, even though the distances involved hardly justified it. Margo realized he wanted the better sort of people in Charleston to see his fine new coach-and-four, with his questionable coat-of-arms and motto painted so conspicuously on it. The coach was blue, but Margo had to admit it was every bit as beautiful as the Gilded Coach of her dreams.

"I really feel rather embarrassed riding in such a decorative vehicle driven by a liveried coachman and lackey," Margo told Lewis. "To make

144

matters even more absurd, the front two horses are not even attached to the whiffletree. They merely prance out in front, while the second two horses do all the work." Margo could hardly imagine what her father would have given for just one of the idle horses.

"The unnecessary horses out in front," Margo continued, "remind me of a painting I saw at the Middletons. The picture showed four horses pulling a cart across the sky. They said they had bought it on one of their many European tours."

"That's a copy of a famous painting by Guido Reni showing Apollo's chariot racing across the sky," Lewis explained. "But don't say cart, say chariot. That's a more elegant word than cart, more suitable for a god."

"Did you notice that the horses are not harnessed to the chariot and therefore serve no purpose except for show, just like Colonel Pinckney's forward team?"

"It's a funny thing, Margo," Lewis said, "that the families who make the greatest display of wealth often have the greatest debts. Many of them owe so much they are really no richer than the poorest indentured servant. However, as long as they keep up appearances, they can keep getting credit."

~

While shopping with Frances in the metropolis, Margo bought two day-caps, two night-caps, five shifts, one sham, a hoop, a quilted petticoat, two flannel petticoats, two pairs of stockings and one odd one, a pair of laced shoes, a short flowered apron, a laced neckerchief, and a bolt of blue silk for an evening gown.

"The seamstresses in Charleston are just as up to date as any in London," Frances tried to convince her skeptical companion. Margo also bought a large copper bath tub and two copper buckets. In the well-stocked book shop she bought a just-imported copy of Richardson's *Clarissa*, not for herself but for the widow Horton. Margo had long since outgrown Richardson's tedious letters, but she was sure that the widow Horton had not.

~

Margo could not speak French, but she did learn to pronounce the many French words that had crept into stylish English conversation. She had to learn *épatant, de rigueur, en passant, s'il vous plaît, pas de quoi, bon mot, formidable,* and a score of other impressive terms. She also had to learn the names of all families in high society, whether or not she was ever going to meet them. As a result of Mrs. Horton's careful coaching, she had little trouble with English names such as Bull, Hopton, Middleton, Fenwick, Drayton, and Gibbes, but she had more difficulty with Huguenot names such as Manigault, pronounced Manigo; Huger, pronounced U.G.; and Prioleau, pronounced Pree-o-lo.

In Charleston, Margo saw her first play, for which Frances had reserved tickets weeks in advance.

"Why didn't you get a ticket for Lewis?"

"I knew he would enjoy it, but *The Recruiting Officer* is said to be a very bawdy play, and it would be unbecoming for a man of the cloth to be seen at it." Margo herself was a bit shocked at the risqué performance. Lewis did not attend the play, but he did join the ladies after the show at the sumptuous Shepheards Tavern, where they were served a Lucullian feast.

The next day, while Margo and Lewis were window shopping, Margo was stopped in her tracks by two Dresden figurines. "Look," she gasped, "those are two of the passengers in my Gilded Coach. See, they are both dressed like shepherds. Not like any shepherds I've ever seen, because all the ones I've ever seen were barefoot and in rags, like the shepherds in the Nativity Scene every Christmas at our church. These are dressed in silk and satin and are wearing white wigs. Such costumes wouldn't last long while guarding sheep. Even their white crooks wouldn't last long."

"No, but such costumes are most suitable for playing shepherd. The custom has been very popular among English lords and ladies for more than a century. They read poetry and sing pastoral songs. Perhaps Mrs. Horton read you this one:

> Come live with me and be my love,
> And we will all the pleasures prove,
> That hills and valleys, dales and fields,
> And all the craggy mountain yields.

I think that is the way it runs. The shepherd promises to make her a bed of roses and a gown of finest wool."

"That's fine enough. But is my Gilded Coach going to bring them their picnic lunch?"

"They don't worry about things like that. It makes them feel very much a part of the spring. It is their escape from the artificial life at court into an equally artificial pastoral life."

"If you insist, Lewis, my Dear, I will go live with you and be your love," Margo agreed, "but only in the parsonage. It gets cold sleeping at night with the sheep."

～

Although Margo was still officially in mourning and wearing black, Frances had a new evening gown fitted for her for a very important engagement. She had made an appointment with Jeremiah Theus, Charleston's leading portraitist, to paint a picture of Margo as a wedding present for Lewis. Margo noted at once that Theus spoke a Swiss dialect much like her own, but she did not mention it, because she was now a Huguenot of ancient lineage, not a Swiss peasant.

"The portrait looks rather formal and a bit stiff," Margo confided to Frances.

"Perhaps it's that way because Theus has been told that you are to be a parson's wife."

Later Margo observed that most of Theus' grand ladies looked very stiff and formal. She suspected that sometimes the luxurious costumes had been filled in imaginatively either before or after the lady sat for the artist.

～

Even more important for Frances than making Margo into a grand lady was making her into a good Anglican.

"We should attend church together regularly. I will advise you when to stand, sit, and genuflect."

"Genu what?"

"Genuflect. Kneel in a proper Anglican fashion. You will be doing a lot of it. And we should join the choir so you can learn the most frequently sung hymns."

Margo also read scripture in the family's evening devotions. Still more important was instruction in the *Book of Common Prayer*, from which Margo quickly learned the Apostles' Creed, the Confession, and other soul-saving items. Frances even asked a nearby parson's wife to invite them to tea so that the new convert could see how she was to act later on when she, too, was a parson's wife.

To impress Margo with the importance of the Anglican Church in South Carolina, Frances took her to see the new church then being built at Sheldon. Leaving home at daybreak with two armed black retainers, the young women rode all day to reach Sheldon, where they were graciously received by some of Frances' Middleton cousins.

The next morning they rode over to the construction site, where a dozen massive brick columns were being erected. The floor of the church had been paved with cobble stones, and thick brick walls were rising around it. Margo was amazed at the number of laborers, all black, and at the speed with which they worked under their black drivers.

On the way back from Sheldon the two travelers stopped at a well tended garden. What caught Margo's attention was a peculiar stone monument, an ivy-covered obelisk, standing at least eight feet high. When Margo asked its meaning, Frances explained that the bereaved husband could not bear to have his bride buried in the cold, cold ground. Instead, he had the coffin placed upright above ground and had it surrounded by stones. Thus her spirit could roam at night in the garden she so dearly loved.

When Margo next saw Lewis, she was ecstatic about the handsome Middleton mansion.

"Do you know how the Middletons came by their fortune?" Lewis asked.

"By planting rice, I assume."

"No, by selling Indian slaves to the Sugar Islands. All they had to do was to arm a tribe and sic it on another. After that there were plenty of slaves real cheap. Not fond of work, the Indians did not last long under

148

the lash, but most did live long enough to pay back their cost and a bit more to boot."

"How horrid!"

"The greatest fortunes around here were made in trade. Later, many merchants branched into planting because it brings more status, since status depends largely on the number of slaves one possesses. It just isn't possible to control a hundred house servants."

"Then we Delegals must have some status, having as many slaves as we do," Margo said.

"But nothing like the Fenwicks. John Fenwick came from an established family in Stanton and started planting rice in a big way and did very well, but the better part of his wealth he inherited from his older brother Robert, a Red Sea man."

"A Red Sea man?"

"He used to capture Moslem vessels in the Indian Ocean and the Red Sea."

"You mean he was a pirate?"

"Not exactly. He never looted Christian vessels, unless we were at war with their country at the moment. Moslem ships are fair game, and the Moslems feel the same way about Christian ships."

"Did he have to sail all around the Cape of Good Hope?"

"All the way to Mozambique and beyond. I see that you remember Mrs. Horton's geography lessons very well."

Lewis continued to kiss his betrothed in a dignified manner, although Margo wished he would go further. In rural Switzerland it was no disgrace if a fiancée became pregnant, the marriage merely had to be advanced to some convenient date, preferably before the child's birth. The engagement was the legal bond, always well witnessed, while the marriage was just the blessing and the exchange of gifts. However, realizing that a churchman should not violate the rule of chastity, Margo refrained from ever tempting her well-behaved fiancé.

12

Drum Plantation

The marriage was delayed for two reasons. Margo had not yet finished her mourning, and Lewis had not yet taken his holy orders. When these two requirements were finally fulfilled, the marriage took place in Saint Philip's Church in Charleston and was followed by a lavish wedding feast of greenturtle soup, shad roe, venison, and many other delectable dishes, accompanied by many vintages of Madeira. The best of these was "Habersham's Rainwater". It was said that James Habersham had his wine transported from Madeira to London, then to Charleston, back to London, and then, properly matured by the extended motion, to Charleston again.

The marriage ceremony was performed by Commissary Garden and attended by all the aristocracy of the Low Country. From Georgia came John Milledge and Noble Jones, who had thought up an official excuse for bringing his scout boat to Charleston. Both men were resplendent in military uniform. Perhaps they were afraid that their civilian attire, while good enough in Georgia, might look too rustic in South Carolina. The senior widow Horton, who happened to be visiting her son in Charleston, also attended. She smiled mischievously at Margo, obviously proud of her little Galatea's social progress and her own complicity. Margo also saw John Stout on a back pew with a sturdy and plainly dressed farmwife, but Stout had the tact not to attend the reception.

The *South Carolina Gazette* reported:

Yesterday at St. Philips Church were joined in holy matrimony the Rev. Lewis Middleton Delegal and the widow Margaret Bacques, whose husband, the late Captain Gabriel Bacques, lost his life in the recent war against Spain. The

150

widow Bacques is descended from an illustrious Huguenot line, including . . . .

Then followed a list of names of which Margo had never heard.

Directly after the ceremony the young couple proceeded to the Anglican parsonage at Pondee in a dugout canoe laden with wedding gifts. The craft was rowed by six husky rowers, who were aided by a strong flood tide, so the journey took only a few hours.

"I'm truly enjoying the songs," Margo said, relaxing in Lewis' arms.

"English hymns sung with African rhythms. You are going to hear a lot of them."

Margo was delighted with the parsonage, which was ample and well-appointed but more a manse than a mansion. It would have been very much at home in an English parish, being built of stone rather than of brick, as all other buildings thereabout were. It was only a mile from *Drum Plantation*, Lewis' small but productive rice plantation.

The servants had arrived ahead of them to put everything in order. Awaiting Margo at Pondee was the copper bathtub she had bought in Charleston.

"Have it filled right away with very hot water," she ordered Patience.

"Yassam," Patience answered. It was the only Gullah word in her large English vocabulary. She immediately had the tub filled with very hot water brought up in the copper buckets from the cauldron in the kitchen, which was in a separate outbuilding. Many loads were needed to fill the tub, and others to keep the water hot. This was the most luxurious moment of Margo's life, and she was extravagant with the bath salts. She remembered how her mother used to sponge her three children every Saturday night in order of age, they standing in a basin containing a gallon or two of warm water.

"How far I have come," she said to her mirror. "Why me? What did I do to deserve all this?"

~

After a light supper served by two servants, Lewis and Margo retired to their quarters and parted to put on their shifts.

151

Margo was pleased that the parsonage was empty and well-locked so no Schneider women could interrupt them. She entered the bedroom first and climbed into bed, hoping that Lewis' kisses would not be so restrained as up to now.

Lewis followed in his night shirt and joined her on their bridal bed. Making sure that their mosquito net was properly hung, the young clergyman took out his Bible and read from the Song of Songs:

Behold, thou art fair, my love; thou hast doves' eyes within thy locks: thy hair is as a flock of goats, that appear from Mount Gilead. Thy teeth are like a flock of sheep that are even shorn, which came up from the washing; whereof every one bear twins, and none is barren among them. Thy lips are like a thread of scarlet, and thy speech is comely; thy temples are like a piece of pomegranate within thy locks. Thy two breasts are like two young roes that are twins, which feed among the lilies.

The groom left the bed and knelt before it like a holy shrine. "The Lord hath given us five senses for our enjoyment," he said, "and we should enjoy all five of them." He then dug his hands into Margo's rich glossy hair and loosened it, taking delight in its slightly perfumed scent. Next he brushed her lips with his, sucking her lower lip into his to enjoy its taste all the better. After that he laid his head on her breast to hear the pleasing sound of her pounding heart. Then he relished the feel of her cheeks and throat. Lighting two more candles, he removed her shift, with a bit of assistance, and then threw back the covers to enjoy the sight of her beautiful body. Having indulged all his five senses, he dropped his night gown and climbed, partially pulled, into the bed.

Margo thrilled at the feel of his firm body pressed full length so tightly against hers. His kisses, no longer those of a parson, sent tingles up and down her spine. His right hand cupped her left breast, and Margo felt her nipple harden as his thumb gently caressed it. When his hand explored her inner thigh, her mind went blank and left her body to function on its own. The whole sky filled with fireworks. Later, during the afterglow, she understood what the Bible means when it says that man and wife are of one flesh.

~

Margo slept late. Upon awakening, she saw Lewis already dressed in his riding togs.

"You look more like a hunter than a clergyman," she teased.

"Dress the same way, my Love. Frances tells me you have a new riding habit. We have places to go."

While Margo was complying with his command, she stopped to reflect. *This is the first time Lewis has ever given me an order, as Gabriel always did. Previously, he always asked me what I wished to do. Will it be different now that I have promised to obey? I doubt it. He's always so considerate.*

After a filling breakfast, the newly-weds set out for their plantation, she sidesaddle on Pegasus and he astride a lesser mount, thus putting their faces on the same level with the result that Lewis could kiss his bride's cheek whenever the spirit so moved him, as it often did. The ride was about a mile through pine forests.

"Why are the church and the parsonage so far from the landing?" Margo asked, patting Pegasus on his withers.

"To keep them as far away as possible from any swamp or rice field because malaria is caused by miasmic vapors generated by stagnant water. That's why they call it *mal aria*, bad air. Most wealthy planters send their families to New England for the entire summer."

When the young equestrians arrived at Drum Plantation they were greeted by Elisha, the distinguished looking black foreman-manager, who went through the gesture of "pully wool an' scratchee foot."

"Where did he learn to do that?" Margo asked.

"Good manners," Lewis explained. "When our Anglo-Saxon ancestors spoke to their Norman conquerors they had to doff their caps and make curtsies. Since the Negroes wear no caps, they pull at their forelocks and draw back their right foot as a curtsy."

As soon as Elisha had moved on, Margo remarked, "I didn't know there were any black plantation managers."

"There aren't many, Sweetheart," Lewis answered, "but Elisha's people have managed plantations for us ever since we were in Barbados. He is one of the most successful planters on the delta. A neighbor of ours, a very competent planter, keeps his books for him and finds everything being well run. Starting next season I'll keep the books myself."

"Or perhaps I can do it?"

"A good idea, my Dear. It's a rather small plantation. You see, our family follows the law of primogeniture."

"What's that?"

"The oldest son inherits all the land in order to keep the estate intact. The younger brothers get the choice of being military officers or clergymen, and the father buys his landless sons either a commission or a prebend. Since I was not exactly officer material, he procured me this 'living' at Pondee and threw in Drum Plantation as a bit of outside income. As you know, my older brother Edward inherited the family estate on the Santee."

~

"Did slaves have to dig all those ditches and build all those dikes?" Margo asked. "Why couldn't you use oxen or water buffalo?"

"Slaves are cheaper in the long run," Lewis answered. "When they aren't digging they can fell trees, plant, harvest, row boats, and do other things that most water buffalos can't do."

Margo was shocked that human beings could be valued lower than oxen, yet she said nothing.

Oblivious of Margo's displeasure, Lewis pointed to the elaborate floodgates.

"All of seasoned cypress wood," he boasted, "just the heart of the tree. The gates are left open all winter so the river water can cover the fields and leave a heavy deposit of fertile silt, just as in Egypt."

"Do the gates work automatically?"

"Yes, after they have once been set. The ground is dry when the seed is planted. The seed's no longer broadcast, it's drilled into the ground

154

with a seed-drill, a machine recently invented by an English agronomist named Jethro Tull."

"What's an agronomist?"

"An expert on crop production," Lewis answered. Margo reached in her pocket, took out her notebook, and added the word.

"When you see a field of ripe rice," Lewis continued, "it's so thick that you would think the seed was broadcast, not planted in regular rows."

"I thought rice grew in water." Margo remembered pictures of Chinese coolies knee deep in water.

"That's just during the sprout and stretch flows. Because the young rice blades have difficulty competing with faster-growing weeds, the fields are flooded a second time and the weeds are drowned and the rice is stretched. That means it has to grow fast to get air and sun. Despite the stretch flow it is a laborious crop because the remaining weeds have to be hoed by hand." Lewis simulated the task of hoeing weeds.

"Notwithstanding all the work," Lewis continued, "it's still six or seven times more productive than corn or wheat. Because rich silt is added every winter, the fields never lose their fertility. The planters can succeed even if hurricanes knock out a trunk or two every three or four years."

"What's a trunk?"

"It is the whole sluice," Lewis explained, "including the two flood gates at either end and the wooden culvert between them."

"How long does it take to replace one?"

"Weeks and weeks, and at great expense. Cypress boards are expensive now because all the big trees on navigable streams have been cut down."

"Why don't you let the Salzburger carpenter George Kogler prefabricate one for you to hold in reserve?" Margo then described the way Kogler cut boards that could be assembled into a house.

"Do you think he could do the same for a rice-field trunk?" Intrigued by the idea, Lewis made a careful sketch of his latest trunk, giving the exact measurements of every board, every dowel hole, and every mortised joint. Margo sent this sketch, along with instructions and cordial greetings, to Kogler, who asked Pastor Gronau to translate the instructions for him.

A month later Habersham's sloop delivered the crated pieces to Charleston. From there they were rafted to the Pondee landing and stored in the Drum Plantation barn.

~

Back at the parsonage after their first visit to Drum Plantation, Margo found Lewis' amorous routine less ritualistic than previously, but equally fulfilling. When his lips brushed against hers, they reached the unplumbed depths of her heart, and when his mouth pressed hungrily on her lips, she heard her heart hammering in her chest with the same intensity as his. Margo felt her bones dissolve. She was no longer an individual being, but just half of a whole. When the ecstasy finally ended and she was lying relaxed in Lewis' tight embrace, she was satisfied that the passion of the first night had not just resulted from long abstinence but would recur forever.

Freeing herself from Lewis' embrace, Margo put her head under the covers and explored his left thigh. She soon felt the jagged scar he had sustained in the War of Jenkin's Ear. Caressing the scar tenderly, she kissed it several times.

"It's really lovely," she said out loud. "I wonder if I married you so I could see what the surgeon was hiding from me?"

Lewis did not answer. He was still fast asleep.

After letting Lewis sleep a bit longer, Margo got up and started to dress, Lewis stopped her.

"Please don't cover your bosom. Let me enjoy looking at it."

"If that's what you want, my Dear." She let him gaze, thinking it would excite him sexually, but she soon saw that her breasts gave him aesthetic more than sensual enjoyment. He delighted when she reached up to get something from a shelf, with one arm or with two, and he delighted equally when she knelt down to pick up her shoe from the floor. No matter what her posture, her breasts always assumed a beautiful shape.

"I wish I were a sculptor and able to give permanence to such beauty," Lewis would say, after feasting his eyes.

In a short time Lewis and Margo developed their own private vocabulary. Out of a sense of loyalty, Margo was careful not to introduce any intimate words or expressions she and Gabriel had shared. (Such care was not needed, since their love-talk had been in German). Instead, she let Lewis choose most of the words, many of them from mythology or literature. In all cases, they were too obscure for anyone else to understand and could therefore be used without fear of being overheard.

~

Margo hardly knew how to enjoy her new-found leisure. She wanted desperately to work because so much had to be done, but custom would not allow her to do it. Instead, she had to call a servant and supervise the task, which she could have done so much faster and better by herself. Fortunately, no one, not even the servants, knew how hard she was working on the plantation account books. Even if they saw her sitting at her desk, they would not accuse her of working. Once Lewis had overheard a black visitor ask one of his slaves,

"Yo massa ebber wuck?"

"My massa ent make fuh wuck. He jess sit at he desk all day an take he pledger."

All that season Lewis had been at his desk long hours every day filling out birth, baptismal, marriage, and death reports to Commissary Garden, as well as doing tedious parish business.

"Commissary Garden himself," Lewis confided to Margo, "is having his woes at this time. George Whitefield is in Charleston fulminating against the corruption and ungodliness of the Anglican Church."

"Fulminating means thundering?" Margo wrote the word down in her notebook.

"Exactly. The Dissenters, especially the Congregationalists, Quakers, Presbyterians, and Huguenots, are delighted to lend him their pulpits to rant and rave against the Established Church, whose members have recently so subtly and effectively excluded them from all political power. The worst of Whitefield's supporters against Garden was Hugh Bryan."

"I once bought a cow from Bryan," Margo said. "I heard that he taught all his slaves to read so they could read the gospels."

"That he did, to the disgust of all the planters. But he has lost credence now."

"How so?" Margo asked.

"He announced he was going to walk on water; but, when everyone gathered to watch him, the water failed to hold him up. I think he's really mad."

"I wish everyone would leave Garden alone so he could tend his garden," Margo said. "I understand he is a great horticulturist and florist. They say that the gardenia was named for him. He must have bred it or imported it."

"Not exactly true," Lewis interrupted, "the famous Charles Town botanist is Dr. Alexander Garden, the son of Commissary Alexander Garden, the clergyman."

"I suppose that, now that he has digraced himself, Bryan won't be of much help to Whitefield in his feud against Garden," Margo suggested.

"That doesn't matter much, because Whitefield can sway any crowd he preaches to. As soon as he opens his mouth people begin crying, weeping, and wailing about their sins."

"I saw that at Frederica when he preached there," Margo agreed. "Everyone was wild, even the Swiss and Germans, who probably hadn't understood a word of what he said."

On their way home Margo saw a group of merry field hands dragging a large log, some five feet long and nearly two feet in diameter.

"What are they doing?" Margo asked.

"Bringing in the yule log," Lewis answered.

"Why such a big one, and so green?"

"So it will burn longer. As long as the yule log burns, the fieldhands don't have to work. That's why they cut such a green one. It'll take a lot of kindling to get it started."

Margo thought she recognized the melody. It sounded somewhat like *Deck the halls*, but with a strange rythm. The words were incomprehensable to Margo, and perhaps to the singers as well.

～

Determined to familiarize herself with Charleston politics, Margo dragged Lewis to a coffee house every time they went to town. He could not complain, because in return she would take a piano lesson from

Charles Theodore Pachelbel, thus freeing her husband to attend the banquets of The Right Worthy and Amicable Order of Ubiquarians, of which he was honorary chaplain. Pachelbel was the son of Johann Pachelbel, who greatly influenced Johann Sebastian Bach.

More exciting for Margo were the receptions at the governor's mansion, to which Lewis was eligible through his birth, correct religious persuasion, and Oxford training. For some reason the Governor, James Glen, often saw fit to introduce Margo to other Huguenots, especially to the artisan John Paul Grimké and the printer Peter Timothy. Although both gentlemen spoke impeccable English, Margo at once detected a faint German accent.

Boltzius had mentioned Timothaeus, the German printer, whom Benjamin Franklin had chosen to edit the German edition of his newspaper. Mrs. Timothy was understood to be from the Netherlands, which showed how the word Dutch was misunderstood at the time. Margo was pleased to be one of the Huguenots because it was thought that, because they could speak French, they must be of the nobility or at least of the higher classes. In time she noticed that they were mostly artisans.

Whenever she went to the city, Margo took organ lessons from John Saltar, the organist at Saint Philips. There she met Eliza Lucas, a charming young woman who had recently married one of Frances' Pinckney cousins. She had been born in the West Indies but educated in England. Energetic, intelligent, and imaginative, she not only cultivated herself but also cultivated several hundred acres of rice at Wappoo Creek Plantation. Margo was relieved to learn that not all the ladies of the Low Country were as insipid as her sister-in-law Frances.

"I'm surprised," Lewis remarked, "that you are so fond of Eliza. It's obvious that you are jealous of her, and envy usually causes hate. The Romans wisely had one word, *invidia*, to denote both hate and envy. But Eliza's attainments seem to cause you more admiration than envy."

"What I admire," Margo said, "is the breadth of her interests. She can manage her rice and indigo business one day, and the next day she plays a harpsichord duet with Pachelbel in the afternoon and makes shrimp nets in the evening."

"There's only one thing I don't like about Eliza. She brags too much about her husband. Anytime she has an audience, she sings his praises. He is the kindest, most loving, and thoughtful husband in the world."

"Perhaps," Lewis suggested, "she feels she must prove that their May and January marriage is satisfactory. You know, he is a generation older."

"I know, one of the Pinckney girls was Eliza's closest friend, and the late Mrs. Pinckney treated her like a daughter."

"Next time she starts bragging about the colonel, why don't you start singing my praises as the kindest, most loving, and thoughtful husband in the world?"

"But then we would have a real *Maennervergleich*."

"What's that?"

"A husband comparison. Today we try to keep our children from saying, 'My daddy's bigger than your daddy,' but long ago even adults behaved that way. In the Siegfried story, which is still sung back home, the two queens, Kriemhild and Brunhild, both claim to have the best husband. The squabble becomes nasty. Brunhild argues that her husband, Gunther, must be the better man because he is freeborn whereas Siegfried is a bondsman. Kriemhild retaliates by saying that Siegfried is not a serf, as he has pretended to be, but freeborn. Besides, it was he, not Gunther, who first deflowered Brunhild. It's not surprising that all this led to Siegfried's murder."

～

Because of her enforced leisure, Margo had time to play the organ in the Pondee church, a skill she learned from the prior organist there, now retired, and was honing with Saltar's help. In a few months she was supplying the music at divine services. Improvising on the organ became her greatest joy. After playing several pieces by Bach, she would let her fingers range over the keys to see what new chords they could discover. Sometimes she would happen upon a chord that brought cosmos out of chaos and answered all her spiritual problems. How did I live before discovering this outlet? she wondered.

Margo's fascination for polyphonic music went back to that fateful day when the Gilded Coach pulled into her meadow. To be sure, she was more impressed then by the liveried servants and by the silver dishes, but she was also affected by the songs the young shepherds sang. One of the young ladies sang an aria solo, then the other one joined her in a duet. Next the two young gentlemen joined them in a quartet. It was the first time Margo had heard four-voice song.

This ancient memory reminded her of the Englishman who visited Ebenezer while she was there spinning.

"It's a funny thing," the perplexed visitor commented, "when four Englishmen sing together, they all sing the same song, but when four Salzburgers sing together, they sing four different songs."

~

Margo's second greatest joy after music was her flower and vegetable garden. At first she only asked for a flower garden, knowing it would not be refused. Then she gradually introduced vegetables in quantities far too great for her table. She was growing them for the slave quarters, where the diet consisted mostly of rice and salted side meat and sometimes chitterlings and pigs feet. She knew that green vegetables were necessary for health, as she had learned first hand during her own recuperation from scurvy.

"Many of the children in the village look undernourished," she told Lewis, "they need a better diet." Margo was not allowed to do any of the physical labor in the garden herself. Even Patience resolutely refused to stoop to such an undignified role. Margo had to stand by idly while supervising some incompetent field hand.

Margo always felt a sense of guilt when seeing the discrepancy between the lives of the slaves and those of their owners, and she tried to estimate how many hours a pregnant black woman had to work in the hot sun to provide her with a new evening gown. To her way of thinking, Charleston imported too much silk and satin and not enough osnaburg, the cheap cloth worn by the slaves.

"I would gladly give up my new wardrobe to supply our people with warmer clothing during the cold winter months," Margo assured Lewis. "This is going to be a cold winter."

"How do you know?" Gabriel asked.

"By the Canada geese," Margo explained. "They are coming south early this year. I heard them honking almost all last night.

"I know there is little I can do," Margo sighed. "But at least we could give our people some warm clothes for the winter. Of course, I would appear ungrateful if I complained of the system."

"That you would, indeed," Lewis agreed.

"I don't like all this luxury and waste at the expense of the poor workers. Couldn't we share the income a little more fairly?"

"If we treated our people any better, our neighbors and parishioners would resent it. They would think we are trying to upset the social order. You will just have to bear your cross as I bear mine."

"What cross?"

"The cross of having to pretend I believe everything I preach. I accept the spirit of Christianity and the beatitudes, but I don't think the Bible is the word of God. It's a splendid book and contains some great wisdom, but some of the Old Testament is rather primitive and barbaric. I don't believe God is a jealous God or that He is so concerned about His good name. In fact, I don't really believe in an anthropomorphic god."

By now Margo seldom had to ask Lewis the meaning of even a five syllable word. She had acquired nearly his entire vocabulary and was using words he had never heard. Besides that, she had bought Samuel Johnson's dictionary and was trying to learn all the words in it. Lewis had noted that an unduly large number of her exotic words began with an A or B.

Lewis continued, "I mean a god made in the image of man, with so many of man's faults, such as wrath and vengeance. For me, my God is all love and spirit. So think how hypocritical I feel when I teach our little Sunday schoolers about the Holy Ghost and all the legends about Jesus."

"Then at least we can share our inner conflicts together."

∼

On a bright sunny winter day, while Margo was working in her garden (i.e. directing the work in her garden), Lewis interrupted her and pointed at a little teal flying full speed over their heads.

"Something must be chasing him," Lewis surmised. "Teals are about the fastest birds in the world, and this one is beating all records."

After the little duck had flown about a quarter of a mile and almost out of sight, Lewis and Margo saw him make an abrupt u-turn and come back over their heads. In a moment they saw what caused him to change direction. A duck hawk had blocked his path and pursued him a short distance. The teal then flew about a third of a mile from where the spectators were watching before making another u-turn. He had again been blocked by a duck hawk.

"The poor bird is trapped. If he keeps flying back and forth between the two conspirators he'll run out of breath and be caught by the hawks. These duck hawks, the *falco peregrinus*, are world famous. In the Middle Ages only the high nobility were permitted to hunt with them. When the first hawk blocked his path, the faster-flying teal should have made a right-angle turn and evaded them, but he wasn't that smart."

Meanwhile the teal was tiring, and the two falcons were closing in. After the teal had made about six attempts to flee, one of the falcons climbed a bit and waited. Then as the teal passed under it, the falcon stooped and struck its victim, which fell in a cloud of feathers and nearly hit the ground before the other falcon swooped and grasped the prey and the two raptors flew away together to find a tall tree to enjoy their hard-earned meal.

"What a shame such a beautiful bird had to die just to maintain two hawks for one more day," Margo complained.

"We kill ducks just for the fun of it," Lewis said. "They do it because they have to."

~

One day Lewis saw Margo squatting next to a rice rick.

"What in the world are you doing?"

"Feeding a doodlebug," Margo answered, dropping an ant into a little funnel-shaped hole in dry sand under the rick.

"Do you think that a dignified thing for the wife of an Anglican minister to be doing?"

"Dignified or not, it's still a lot of fun. Just look how energetically the doodlebug is throwing up the sand."

Lewis watched the sand being thrown up from the bottom of the hole. The ant was trying desperately to climb up the sandy wall of the hole, but the sand thrown up by the antlion kept dragging it down again. All this time the predator's soft body was covered by the sand, leaving only its pincers exposed for throwing up the sand and eventually catching the unfortunate ant.

"Don't you think that a rather childish pastime?"

"Not really. We didn't have doodlebugs when I was a child in Switzerland, and I am just making up for what I missed."

∼

Not far from the doodlebugs was the slave cemetery. Despite Lewis' objections, the graves were decorated with bottles and pottery, all of them broken. Margo was far from impressed by the decor. She thought she recognized a broken porcelain teapot that had disappeared recently from the pantry, still unbroken. Seeing time-worn Aunt Sarah nearby, she asked, "Why are all the bottles and pots broken, Aunt Sarah?"

"Dat's so nobody won't steal um," the old woman answered, straightening up her apron.

"But what good are they all broken up like that?" Margo asked.

"Dey all broke up here on de uth, fuh sho, but in heb'm day all be put back togedder."

One day when returning home, Margo saw one of the slave women sneaking away from her doorstep. Curious to know why, she looked under the bottom step and found a small leather bag. Having no idea what it might be, she took it to Maum Edith, a superannuated pipe-smoking crone, who said it was a "root" or a ' han'(hand)." Edith sent her to Sarah, who was a renowned conjurer. Sarah admitted she did not know the contents, but she assumed it was graveyard dirt dug up on the full of the moon. The rest was known only to the sorceress herself.

Maum Edith endorsed the power of such fetishes.

"Someone put a han' unner Diana house and she loss her nature, an' she loss her husban', too. She fine de han' and brung it to me. She tink de han' be leff by Lydia, de woman her man leff her for. I make

Diana a mo' better han' and she put it unner Lydia her house, an' Lydia she loss her nature. Diana she got her nature back, an' her husban', too."

Margo had recognized the woman who planted the 'han' under her doorstep, but she could not imagine why she wanted to harm her mistress. She summoned Celia for an explanation. Terrified and weeping, Celia admitted to leaving the hex.

"I leff it day 'caze I know you wants chilluns. Aunt Sarah say dis han' make any woman have chilluns."

～

Margo's gnawing fear was that she was sterile, despite the 'han' left under her doorstep. She knew that Stout was not responsible for her infertility in Savannah because he had sired a family back in Saarbruecken and another one more recently in South Carolina. She hardly thought her virile Gabriel was to blame, either. She did not know why God was punishing her by making her barren. She resented her monthly periods now not so much because they curtailed her activities as because they confirmed that she was not yet fulfilling her main function in life.

Margo felt guilty when she saw how much emphasis her new family placed on their illustrious ancestors. She knew they were equally interested in illustrious descendants, and she was afraid she would disappoint them. She wished she had a mother with whom to discuss this matter.

～

Margo was not always so glum. She was almost always happy when Lewis was present, which was most of the time. One evening after grace, Lewis raised his glass and said,

> Drink to me only with thine eyes
> And I will pledge with mine . . .

Margo immediately responded with,

> Or leave a kiss but in the cup
> And I will not look for wine.

This was the beginning of a game they often played. Playing was easy, for Lewis had read more poetry than theology at Oxford and Mrs. Horton had taught Margo all the poems she knew. Besides that, they could cheat by freshening up their memories from their personal anthologies. After all, the pleasures of the mind are even greater, Margo decided, than those of the body.

~

On their second visit to Drum Plantation, Margo heard a loud singing and shouting coming from Rice Hope, the neighboring plantation.

"What's all that racket?"

"That's a 'claying' or 'singing'," Lewis answered. "The field hands are 'claying' the rice seeds. That means they have covered the seeds with wet clay and are dancing on them to make the clay stick. Then, after the clay-covered seeds are dried and broadcast and the water is let in, they stay down and don't flow away with the water. It is an old custom from the rice-growing parts of Africa, where most of our slaves came from. The 'singing' doesn't make any sense now, but maybe it did on the Ivory Coast."

"Why isn't there any 'claying' at Drum Plantation?"

"There used to be, but now that we have the Jethro Tull drill, it's no longer necessary. Our way is much more efficient, even if less romantic."

After accompanying Lewis on his inspection of the sluices and flood-gates, Margo insisted upon visiting "the street", as the slave quarters were called because all the houses faced each other across a well-swept road-way. First she visited the "child house", where all infants and small children were supervised while their mothers were laboring in the field. The work was performed by a thirteen-year-old girl under the supervision of Maum Edith. Although the old woman appeared to be dozing all the time, she heard every cry and every squabble, which she solved with the wisdom of Solomon.

"Wouldn't a younger woman keep the place cleaner?" Margo asked.

"Yes," Lewis answered, "but that would mean one less field hand and therefore less rice."

Margo felt the same about the "sick-house", where infirm and senile old people took care of each other as best they could. Although racked by old-age-pains in all her joints, the supervisor, Maum Rebecca, was amazingly resigned to the Lord's dispensation.

"Ah ain't got but two teet," the decrepit old woman said, "but tank de Lawd dey meet."

~

On their third visit to Drum Plantation, Margo heard a dreadful uproar, even noisier than the "singing". All hands, down to the tiniest child, were blowing horns, beating tin pans, and cracking whips.

"Why all the racket?"

"Just look over there," Lewis answered, pointing toward a black cloud. As the cloud came nearer, Margo saw that it was composed of thousands upon thousands of little birds.

"Ricebirds," Lewis explained. "If we let them land they'll destroy the whole crop. A single bird can empty an ear of rice with just one swoop of its beak."

Frightened by all the pandemonium, the flock flew over to a less well-guarded field a half mile away. Before it left, Elisha fired a load of scatter shot into the flock, and a score of birds fell. Little children gathered them up, and Elisha brought them to his master.

"They're a great delicacy," Lewis assured Margo, "better than four-and-twenty blackbirds. Lot of work plucking them, but well worth the effort. If Patience has the patience to prepare them, we'll have some for breakfast tomorrow. I heard that, when the rice-birds go north in the spring, they put on bright feathers and are very beautiful. The people up there call them bobolinks."

"When I was a child," Margo said, "we used to put a cat's head on a pole and pour bird lime, a kind of glue, on the surrounding branches. Mistaking the cat's head for an owl, the birds would get angry and careless and land on the bird lime. I thought it a mean trick, but they did taste good."

On the next visit to Drum Plantation, Margo saw some children with a basket full of rice mice.

"What are they doing with the mice?" she asked Lewis.

"They are earning their spending money. They get a ha'penny per tail, and their families can eat the mice, which are as tasty as rice birds. The mice are very harmful. They nest in the dikes and come out at night and chew through the rice stalks so they can get at the ears."

～

On their fifth visit to Drum Plantation the young couple found all hands, old and young, male and female, harvesting the crop.

"Why's everybody in such a hurry?" Margo asked.

"The've got to get the crop in before it rains or it could be spoiled. Their rations depend on this crop, so everybody is doing his best."

"May I go and pitch in?" Margo pleaded. "I used to help my parents bring in the wheat."

"No, the hands would take offense. It would shame them in the eyes of the people on the surrounding plantations."

～

On Margo's next visit to Drum Plantation she was alarmed by clouds of smoke.

"Look Lewis, something's burning!"

"Just the stubble. Our people are burning off the fields and dikes to chase out the rabbits. It's their reward for a good harvest."

As they came closer, Margo heard shouting and laughter and saw hundreds of rabbits running back and forth across the fields, while all hands were hurling "throw-sticks" at them. These missiles were pieces of wood about three inches in diameter and a foot long, which could be thrown very accurately. Almost every head of household had a sack nearly full of game.

"All these rabbits are swamp hares, or marsh rabbits as we call them locally. They swim well and also climb trees when necessary."

"They seem much larger than the cottontails I used to skin at Fort Argyle. I feel sorry for them," Margo confessed.

"They all have to die anyway," Lewis reminded her. "It's certainly better to be killed by a throw-stick than to be poisoned by a water moccasin or devoured piecemeal by a hawk. Look at the hawks!"

Margo looked in the direction Lewis was pointing. Dozens of

redtailed and redshouldered hawks were soaring well out of shotgun range but still close enough to catch the rabbits that broke through the human ranks.

"Never pick up a rabbit right away," Lewis warned. "They're covered with fleas. Let'em cool off and the fleas will leave'em. I think the rabbits that got killed today were the lucky ones. They must have to scratch all day long."

~

On another bright day Lewis took Margo to the upland areas of Drum Plantation, which he had never mentioned. Formerly it had been a cattle farm, but now it was planted in indigo, a crop recently introduced from the West Indies chiefly through the efforts of Margo's young friend Eliza Lucas. While the abundant crop was ripening, valiant efforts were being made to complete the vats needed for its treatment. These were huge tubs of cypress planks in which the plants were soaked before being processed. This was a difficult task and required much skill, which a professional was patiently teaching to the Drum Plantation workers.

"The capital investment for all this equipment," Lewis admitted, "is justified only by the generous bounty the government in London pays so we can compete with the planters in the French islands. If the subsidy stopped, the whole industry would shut down."

"I shudder at the thought of how much paperwork the subsidy will cause," the plantation bookkeeper said. "Wouldn't it be easier to cut some of the live oaks along the river and sell the timber to the navy. That's what Eiza has been doing for the past few months."

~

One morning, when Lewis opened the window, he looked out and exclaimed, "If you want to see something unusual, just look out there!"

Margo looked and saw a vast number of ducks even though it was not yet duck season.

"They look to me like summer ducks. What are they doing here?," she asked. "Shouldn't they be up in the woods eating acorns?"

"That's just the hitch," Lewis answered. "For some unknown reason, the entire acorn crop has failed this year." Lewis answered, "Plant-

169

ers are going to have a hard time feeding their hogs. Finding no acorns, the summer ducks have come down to the delta to eat wild rice and also the gleanings from the rice fields. Let's go shoot some."

Margo didn't really wish to shoot such beautiful birds, but she did want Lewis' company. When she agreed, Lewis fetched his shotgun and called to a field hand named Ishmael to ready a dugout. They had gone hardly two hundred yards before some summer ducks rose and Lewis downed one with each barrel. Ishmael jumped into the cold water and tossed one of the victims back into the boat. Then he crossed a dike to find the second, which had fallen at a greater distance. There was a long wait before Ishmael returned, but without a duck.

"Ah shum anna ain' shum. Ah shum anna ain' shum."

"What did he say?"

"He says he saw him and he didn't see him." Margo understood that perfectly. She remembered the gar fish on that first day at Fort Argyle. She saw it, and she didn't see it. She saw it, and she didn't see it. In his succinct language Ishmael had said that, when he went to get the duck, it submerged and then emerged somewhere else and then submerged again, probably to die clinging to the bottom.

13

Perilous Interlude

Life at the parsonage would have continued in its routine way if Commissary Garden in Charleston had not called upon Lewis to perform a clerical function at Augusta, Georgia. Seven of the most important merchants in that busy town had just built a church and wished to have it consecrated. There being no bishops in South Carolina at the time, the chore should have fallen on Pastor Garden, the Bishop of London's commissary, but either he could not go, or he did not wish to.

Lewis accepted the call gladly, finding life at Pondee rather repetitious. When Margo heard he was going to Augusta, she announced she would accompany him, and no amount of argument could dissuade her. They decided to take the overland route on the trail used by the Indian traders between Charleston and Augusta, a frontier settlement standing at the fall line of the Savannah River.

"Because life at Augusta is considered rather primitive," Margo informed her husband, "I'll take no finery. I'll just take two riding habits and one simple dress suitable for church. You should dress similarly." By now she was undisputed master of the wardrobe.

At dawn the young couple left Pondee with their two riding horses and a packhorse led by a young Negro boy named Plato, who rode a small pony much like Margo's Betsy. It was not a marsh tacky, like Margo's mount, but a Chickasaw, a sturdy little beast favored by the Indian traders. Although introduced to Carolina by the Chickasaw Indians, it had been bred far west by the Spaniards of Mexico.

The Delegals and their servant covered much ground before sunset and arrived at a farm belonging to Charleston friends but operated by a Swiss indentured servant and a slave named Zeus. The hovel was squalid, but the host did the best he could and slept in the barn so his guests could use his bed. The next day Lewis asked, "Can you sell me some feed for my horses?"

"No I can't," the farmer answered apologetically. "I'm working on shares, and the contract forbids it." Lewis was astonished at the man's honesty. Surely the owner in Charleston would never know it if he sold a bushel or two of grain.

"Is there nothing I can do?" Lewis asked.

"Perhaps Zeus has some corn to spare. He cultivates a field on Sundays and is free to sell what he doesn't use." Luckily, the Negro was not bound by any restrictive contract and could sell Lewis a couple of bushels. The young traveler was liberal in repaying his hosts, both free and unfree.

The next day the cavalcade was delayed several tedious hours until the ferryman returned to his ferry and took them to a very low and swampy trail on the other side of the river. After many miles of swamp muck, their trail turned into yellow sand. Eventually they reached the pine belt, where the trail was much better.

Although not much more than a child, the packman Plato quickly fed and bedded down their mounts when they finally reached a tavern. It was a wretched dive where the local Swiss and German settlers could find libations and solace.

Fortunately, before the travelers could retire to their uninviting bedroom, an invitation came from Christian Theus, the Reformed minister recently threatened by the Weberites. The black boatman who had rescued Theus from the angry worshippers delivered the invitation, having heard from Plato about the arrival of quality folks.

Theus' parsonage was simple but comfortable, and the guest room adequate. Margo spoke only English to the Swiss divine, who never detected her Swiss origin. From Theus the visitors learned much about Augusta and the church that had just been built there.

"It should be an Anglican Church and have a minister ordained by and supported by that faith. However, since all the seven chief donors are Calvinists, being Scots and Scotch-Irish, we assume that the sermons will be acceptable to a largely Calvinist congregation."

Such an arrangement was not new. Bartholomeus Zauberbuhler, a

Swiss, was ordained in London into the Anglican Church but remained a good Calvinist at heart during his long tenure in Georgia. Margo did not mention her portrait recently painted by the host's brother.

After two more days of riding, the adventurers passed through the southern tip of the sand hills, where the going was much easier in the barren and uninhabited scrub oak wastes. When the Delegals and their little packman finally reached the Savannah River, they were at Fort Moore, a sparsely settled area lying on the left, or Carolina, bank of the river. They saw only about a dozen houses there, and they heard later that the Indian traders preferred to live on the Georgia side where they were safe from their Carolina creditors.

~

Upon crossing the river, the party was met by John Rae, an enterprising Ulsterman. He was the most active of the Big Seven, a conglomerate of traders who enjoyed a virtual monopoly of the Indian trade in the region and were therefore financially able to build the church. Rae was also the chief importer of his Protestant Irish countrymen to the new Georgia lands just ceded by the Indians.

Rae was far more modest in his claims than Riemensperger had been. While admitting that life on the frontier was rough, he offered himself and his colleagues as proof that a man could succeed if he worked hard enough. Skeptics claimed that Rae was bringing in the immigrants just to populate the area between his lands and the Indians. Like his friend Noble Jones, Rae had begun his American career as a scout boat skipper and had aided Oglethorpe in the War of Jenkins' ear. Their names are next to each other in a petition to the King.

The town of Augusta lay almost entirely on the right or Georgia bank of the Savannah River.

"The houses are all built like fortresses," Lewis remarked. "I've heard that each of them sports a cannon. While the Indians are accustomed to the loud reports of their own muskets when they hunt, they are terrified of the thunder of cannons and will flee as soon as one is fired."

~

The first thing Margo noticed in Augusta was the line of soldiers waiting to get into the canteen, while it was mostly the wives and children who were sitting in the new church. A Highlander recognized Margo and doffed his cap.

"By the way," he said, "You remember the Prince of Wurttemberg? Well, he's back in Georgia and up to his old tricks. He joined the British army and was stationed in Boston, but he didn't like it there and deserted. Now he's posing as a Lutheran minister back in Georgia. He tried to get the job here as an Anglican, but Rae and his partners were not fooled."

The brand new church at Augusta was well built, and Lewis felt deep satisfaction in consecrating it. As the new pastor he ordained Jonathan Copp, a man terrified by the wild Indians loitering around town. He was ready to abandon his post at any moment.

Copp's fears were justified. There were rumors of a forthcoming Indian war. The Creeks had been friendly with the English ever since Oglethorpe had made and kept treaties with them, and they depended on the English traders to supply them with guns and powder for shooting deer and hostile Indians. But now a problem had arisen.

Knowing their dependence on the English, the older chiefs had conceded a long strip of land along the right bank of the Savannah, several million acres, to pay the claims of the British merchants for bad debts. The younger braves, however, had never recognized this concession and continued to hunt on the ceded territory. Peace was anathema to the young braves, because an Indian could prove his manhood only in war. A white youth could prove his virility by felling trees, plowing a straight furrow, or making a crop, but the Indians delegated such ignoble tasks to their squaws.

John Rae explained the situation as follows:

"While hunting on land recently granted to one of my Irish immigrants, a renegade hunting party stole one of his horses. Aided by his neighbors, the settler followed the Indians, recognized the horse, whipped the thief, and shot and killed an Indian who resisted."

"Didn't they know that horse-stealing's a crime?" Margo interrupted, remembering the fate of the Fenwicks' groom.

"Not really," Rae answered. "As in the case of wild deer, it's a case of 'Finders keepers, losers weepers'."

The Creek chiefs regretted the violence, over which they had no control, but they warned the whites that they could not restrain their young braves unless the white men punished the killers publicly. That left the Georgia governor in a quandary. If he sided with the Indians he would receive no more settlers, if he sided with the settlers there would be another Indian War, which would be hard to fight.

~

Since Lewis had now completed his ecclesiastical errand, he and Margo were ready to return home and were therefore not greatly concerned about the rumor of war. On the day of their departure they recrossed the Savannah River on one of Rae's boats and sought out the trail by which they had come. Late that evening they came upon an abandoned house, one that had obviously just been deserted. It had been ransacked, and there was not a scrap of food or drink in the larder. Just two mutilated corpses.

While pondering the situation, Lewis heard a sudden howl of war cries, and seven warriors burst into the house and seized and bound him and Margo after a vigorous struggle. It took five warriors to subdue and bind Lewis. The Indians were all very young and very drunk and enjoying themselves immensely. They took only Lewis' boots and jacket, apparently having no use for his trousers. Margo lost most of her clothing to the savages, who must have thought they would impress some Indian maiden.

Meanwhile other Indians had built a fire at the foot of an oak tree in the front yard, kindling it with the cabin's Bible and Arndt's *True Christianity* and feeding it with pine shingles torn from the roof. Margo was terrified, she remembered the charred body of the captive at the war dance near Frederica. Lewis tried to communicate with the captors, but he knew no Creek and they knew no English, and he saw that his and Margo's demise was close at hand. Would they be scalped before being burned, Lewis wondered, for he knew the political value of scalps for

175

ambitious young warriors. He was more concerned about Margo than about himself. Perhaps they would not torture her, since it would not enhance their honor. But some Indians did torture their female captives so their husbands would have to watch the torture and feel disgraced at being unable to prevent it.

The Indian trader Wiggins had explained that the Indians tortured their captives to make them scream. If they did so, their souls would never reach the happy hunting ground. That is why most braves endured the most excruciating torture rather than cry out. Instead of screaming they often chided their captors for not being able to break their silence. Lewis determined to scream as soon as the torture began and thus lessen the Indians' incentive to continue.

Despite the horror of the situation, Lewis made a strange observation. The leader of the braves was blue-eyed. His heavily bespangled crest of hair was jet black, but the shaved sides of his head revealed a blond stubble.

During the victims' mental anguish, the braves had begun their war dance, and their shrieks drowned out all other noises of the night until suddenly there was a burst of fire from the woods. Three of the dancers dropped dead or wounded, and the others, as well as the two guards in the house, fled into the darkness.

Lewis and Margo were unbound by none other than John Stout, now lieutenant in the local militia as well as sheriff. Little Plato, whom the Indians had ignored, had stealthily led Pegasus away to a safe distance and then galloped off down the trail until he found an inhabited cabin. Its owner sent a prearranged signal to his nearest neighbor with his lantern, and he in turn signaled to several other families. Within an hour Stout formed a troop and Plato led it to his master and mistress.

It was later learned that these young braves were among the party that had stolen the horse and had been whipped or shot by Rae's Irishmen. Their honor had been impugned, and only revenge would restore it. It did not matter whether their victim was in any way involved with the insult. It was only necessary to kill a white man in reprisal.

"It may sound strange," Lewis said to Stout, "but the leader of this

176

band was blue-eyed and appeared to be blond under his war paint. Do you suppose he was a mixed breed?"

"No, that was Tulassee, a full-blooded white man," the militiaman answered. "His parents, named Mitchel, were killed when he was so young that he grew up to be an Indian and didn't want to become a white man later on when he had a chance. In fact he was the most Indian of all the Indians I've ever known."

"No Creek Indians have ever crossed into South Carolina to wreak vengeance," Stout remarked. "We were just expecting some runaway Cherokees from up country. I guess you heard about Fort Loudoun?"

"Not yet," Lewis answered.

"The Cherokees besieged the fort, and the starving garrison surrendered the fort under promise of safe conduct. But on the way back they were massacred. Lt. Paul Demere, who had just replaced his brother Raymond as commander, was put to the torture."

Margo remembered Paul, who was just a teenager when she left Frederica, a very polite youngster. She grieved for him.

Lewis and Margo recovered their clothes, even those in their pack, and remained that night in the cabin with their rescuers after the massacred couple had received Christian burial. The dead Indians were left to rot. Stout did not remain to receive thanks, but four militiamen stayed behind to escort the couple back to Augusta and three guarded Plato when he led the four horses back to Drum Plantation.

~

During their brief sojourn in Augusta, Margo saw several of the soldiers she had known at Frederica, but she did not speak to them. Most of them were hanging around the canteen, which was being run by none other than Maria Barbara Roth. She was still selling Ebenezer peach brandy, but the soldiers preferred rum. Rum was theoretically illegal in Georgia and Noble Jones had staved in many barrels of it on the Savannah River, but it still flowed freely, especially as a trade good for the Indians.

~

Not wishing to take the trail again, the Delegals belatedly accepted Rae's invitation to travel to Charleston on one of his trading vessels, even though it was heavily laden with skins and furs. Margo remembered watching the very same boat being built at Purysburg by the boat builder Theobald Kieffer.

A short way down the river the twenty-ton vessel stopped at New Windsor, where the famous almanac maker Johann Tobler lived. Tobler had been governor of Appenzell in Switzerland until rejected by the wealthy council members for opposing their treaties with the French, by which the youth of the land was drafted for service in the French army. Tobler, now a justice of the peace, had recently lost a son scalped by the Indians. Rae had suffered the same loss only a year or two earlier.

Margo was most impressed by Tobler's organ, the only one near the Savannah River. Boltzius had tried for years to obtain one, but his wish was never fulfilled. Lewis, still badly shaken by his ordeal, was amazed that his wife could play Tobler's organ with composure so soon after such a dreadful experience.

"I wish the boat would stop at Ebenezer so I could see Gabriel's tomb," Margo said. "But perhaps it is best not to. Barbara Maurer or some other busybody would recognize me and pass the word to Charleston that I am a fallen woman."

The periagua had barely passed Ebenezer before the skipper tried to turn too abruptly at a sharp bend in the river and the overloaded boat capsized. The three passengers, as well as the crew, could all swim, so no lives were lost. The four or five tons of hides and pelts were, however, entirely lost. The heavy cargo being lost, the crew could righten the periagua and bail it out with the help of the passengers and of some Salzburgers living near Abercorn. Fortunately for Rae, his cargo was insured. Having lost his cargo, Rae returned to Augusta after transferring his passengers to another of his Charleston-bound vessels.

When their boat delayed in Port Royal, Lewis called on his sister Frances, whom he had not seen for a long time. She had not yet moved to the new plantation house on the Santee because her husband was still too occupied by the Royal Council. Lewis gave Margo some time to recuperate from her ordeal, and they returned to Drum Plantation just in time for spring planting.

14

Back Home

"Would you like to see something frightening," Lewis asked Margo a few weeks after their perilous journey, just as the full moon was rising. Too proud to say no, she agreed, even though Lewis refused to say what it would be. They mounted their horses and rode along the major canal until reaching the limit of their property. There they crossed a bridge and returned along the other side of the same canal until they were nearly opposite their own slave quarters. Tethering their horses, they continued silently on foot.

"What's that weird wailing and beating of drums?" Margo asked, clutching Lewis' arm.

"You'll see."

After advancing a few hundred yards further on the dike, they reached a point just opposite the little hummock (locally pronounced hammock) at the south end of *Drum Plantation.* By now the strange sounds were much louder and Margo could see a number of people dancing crazily around a fire. Whereas Lewis and Margo were well concealed by the heavy shrubbery growing on the dike, the figures across the canal were clearly visible to them in the silver moonlight because the livestock there had eaten all the underbrush and low branches. Margo was excited by the polyrhythmic hand-clapping and foot-stomping.

"What in the world are they doing?" Margo whispered.

"Voodoo," Lewis answered. "Elisha told me it would take place this full moon, and tonight's the night."

"Are all of our people taking part?"

"No, not all. Elisha, Isaiah, and Debra don't believe in it. And I guess there are others, also, who are too civilized. Most of the participants must have come from other plantations. At least I don't recognize very many faces. Some of our neighbors have mostly African born slaves."

Focusing her field glass, Margo observed the antics of the voodoo priestess. This woman, wearing a red bandanna on her head and many spangles on her dress, had a snake draped around her neck.

"The snake around the woman's neck," Margo said, handing the glass to Lewis, "must be a coachwhip, like the one I saw swallow the rattler."

"I think you're right. And what's the boy giving it from the basket?"

"Looks like chicken eggs."

The priestess appeared possessed by a spirit, for she was jerking violently. Standing at an altar, perhaps on a step, she was taller than most of the shrieking devotees reeling past her to the staccato drum beat. In the bright moonlight Margo could see her shaking a highly decorated gourd, probably a ritual rattle, even though its sound was drowned out by the pounding of the drums. Margo's own heartbeat was keeping perfect time with the deafening drums.

Meanwhile the sorceress, still under the power of a spirit, was shouting some sort of mumbojumbo that synchronized with the wailing of the dancers. Her face was dreadfully contorted.

"What's she sprinkling on the altar?" Margo asked.

"Probably blood. That white stuff she's dropping on the ground must be cornmeal or ricemeal. She's pouring it so carefully she must be making some sort of magic symbol on the ground."

While the witch-woman was doing this, an angry cloud covered the moon and made it hard for Margo to see just what was being revealed by the pale lamp on the alter or by the flickering ceremonial fire. Another acolyte brought the priestess a live chicken, which she hypnotized and handed back to him. The light of the shimmering fire and of the lamp on the altar was mostly blocked by the dancers, but she saw the acolyte burying the chicken alive with his shovel.

"Look at the two men walking barefoot through the fire," Margo whispered. "They don't seem to be getting burned, at least they're not showing any pain."

As the wailing and chanting were reaching a crescendo, a bolt of lightning struck a mighty oak tree, which burst into flames. Two seconds later a noisy thunderclap shook the whole terrain. The brief flash of lightning illuminated the priestess.

"My God," Margo gasped, "that's Patience!"

This wild woman was her prissy and demure servant, who was so attentive every Sunday in the balcony of Pondee Church. Her Christianity could not be more than skin deep. This reminded Margo of their gentle, affectionate, and cuddly Panzer, who was still a "ravenous beast" at heart.

⁓

When the lightning struck, the wailing gave way to screams of terror. The worshippers thought their priestess had summoned the lightning bolt and the subsequent gale and cloudburst. While the voodooists scurried to their quarters, Lewis and Margo ran to their horses and galloped along the canal through the downpour and raging storm.

Upon reaching the bridge, Lewis turned to the right and stopped at Rice Hope, a "working plantation" belonging to Charleston friends. As at Drum Plantation, there was no mansion, just various barns and storehouses and an East-Indian style bungalow for the manager, which included a bedroom for the absentee landowner. The manager, a Scots indentured servant who had recently fulfilled his indenture, was trying to secure what he could from the wind, now at hurricane force. Most of his workers had not yet returned from the voodoo.

Going to the window to judge the storm, Lewis asked,

"Will you please stay here tonight, Margo, in view of your condition?"

"If you insist," Margo agreed reluctantly, making reason overcome impulse. This was the first time she knew Lewis was aware her fervent prayers were going to be answered. The manager's wife led Margo to the owner's bedroom and exchanged her wet clothing for a dry shift.

After sheltering Pegasus in the stable, Lewis resumed his dangerous way through the blustering tempest, guided mainly by the intermittent lightning and trusting the Lord to protect him from the boughs and other debris being hurled across the dikes.

At Drum Plantation he found Elisha directing all hands, including those voodoo votaries who had just returned from the ceremony. They were securing the buildings and corralling the frightened livestock, some

181

of which had been swept into the canal.

~

When daylight returned and the storm waned, the damage turned out to be less than feared. Two majestic oaks had been overturned, many fences were down, and some hogs and lambs had been drowned. Fortunately the deluge had not reached the stored rice crop, and the hogs and lambs could still be butchered.

Lewis ordered a halt to all work and called upon 'his people' to join him in prayer.

"Let us give thanks unto the Lord, who hath shown the power of His wrath for your having worshipped false gods last night but hath not punished Drum Plantation as He should have rightly done if His only begotten Son had not implored Him to show unmerited mercy."

"Amen," said all hands, including those who had been worshipping the devil the previous evening.

The only serious damage caused by the hurricane was a breach in the river dike, where a trunk had been washed away and destroyed.

"It's lucky we have in reserve the trunk you made me order from Kogler," Lewis said, "you deserve a vote of thanks, my Love."

~

Two days after the hurricane, Margo went to watch the trunk being assembled on the landing dock. The boards were so cleverly numbered that the contraption was nearly assembled by the time she arrived. No hardware had been used. All the boards and beams were attached by mortised joints or by dowels. The result looked like a gigantic rat trap. The box, six by six by twenty-five feet, had a raised door at each end. Being too large to lift, it was tumbled into the water and floated down to the breach in the dike like some strange sea monster.

When the trunk reached the breach, it was grounded and held in place by ropes attached to stakes on the shore. There it remained until the flood tide was well advanced. Then all hands began dragging the huge contrivance into place and anchoring it so it would not be carried away when the ebb tide caused the water in the field to run out through the breach.

182

Seeing the water in the field flowing out rather fast, Lewis shouted, "Raise both gates!" There was a brief scurry, and a dozen voices answered, "Gates done be raise."

With the gates raised, the trunk offered less resistance to the ebbing tide. As soon as the tide was low enough and the trunk was at the right level, all hands started throwing large blocks of hard mud under and around it. As the flood tide started again, a race began between man and river; and human muscle won out by laying mud blocks around the trunk on both the river and field side and pounding them down.

When the tide rose a bit higher, Lewis called, "Close the river gate!" After it was shut, only a few trickles of water could be seen seeping under and around the box. Two large barge loads of mud blocks from across the river had been consumed. The victory was well celebrated by a feast of chitterlings, pig's feet, and yellow yams.

❧

Only a few weeks after the new trunk was installed, Margo noticed eel holes in the dam on either side of it. She recognized them because Boltzius had pointed out similar holes in the banks of the new millrace on the Mill River at Ebenezer.

"Uncle Sali used to trap eels," Margo told Lewis, "until he was arrested and severely punished. Peasants were not supposed to eat eels, which were too good for them. An old proverb said *Oel und Fisch, das lass die Herren essen* (Let the lords eat eels and fish). But here in Carolina there are no such restrictions."

Margo wove a cylindrical basket some three feet long and eighteen inches in diameter of sugar cane rinds, being unable to find any reeds such as Uncle Sali had used. She then inserted a funnel of the same material at each end, one of them removable for putting the bait in and taking the eels out. Baiting the trap generously, she set it next to the trunk.

When she returned the next morning, she found four large eels in the basket. Delighted with her success, she took them to the parsonage, where Frances was visiting her.

"Take those nasty snakes out of here," Frances screamed in horror. "No civilized person would eat serpents like that."

Margo wondered what caused the great prejudice against these delicious fish. Finally she remembered the Old Testament law: "Thou shalt not eat fish without scales." She pondered this a moment and then said, "That must have been the reason the Delegals and the Pinckneys never eat catfish either. Being Christians, they cannot eat these unclean fish, while the slaves, being heathens, can do so." She took the booty to Mauma Edith, who accepted it with many thanks.

As soon as Margo had Lewis alone, she complained that her sister-in-law would not let her serve eels.

"Perhaps she's right. Remember poor Lord Randall."

"Who was he?"

"The victim in an old English ballad, whose 'true love' serves him 'eels fried in a pan.' When he gets home he asks his mother to prepare his bed, for all his hounds and hawks, to which he has given the left overs, have died."

"Well, I don't plan to poison anyone. Frances wouldn't eat the eels even if I did poison them. At least the ballad shows that English lords used to eat eels, even if their Carolina descendants won't."

The next day Margo showed her trap to Mauma Edith and suggested that the women in the quarters make and set such traps. A week later Mauma Edith sent word to her mistress to come see the result. Margo was astounded. There were a dozen traps, all just as functional as hers, but much more attractive, being made of a kind of reed she had been unable to find. They were also much better woven. No one had told Margo that the Africans had brought an ancient art of basketry with them, and she never thought to ask about the beautiful baskets she saw for sale at the market in Charleston.

Impressed by the women's skill, Margo also introduced the art of making "bee baskets", as beehives are called in Germany and Holland. She also taught the women the way to catch bees between a bottle and a sugar-covered shingle and then follow them to their swarm.

~

Margo had not been on a beach since leaving Frederica so long before. She only had to ask Lewis once. He invited the Saltonstalls, their nearest neighbors, to join them in an expedition to Kiawah, a barrier island off from Charleston. The neighbors offered their unusually large dugout, and each family provided six rowers, six to row while six rested. Reaching Charleston in a matter of hours, they visited the Hoptons, who had many guest rooms.

The next morning, adding several Hopton children to the expedition, they proceeded by boat to the back of Kiawah Island, where two wagons were waiting to take them across the island to the beach. When blankets were spread on the sand and the picnic lunch was displayed, Margo saw that she was just as well off as the two young couples in the Gilded Coach.

"Let's go look for turtle eggs," Lewis suggested.

"What do you do with turtle legs?" Margo asked.

"Not turtle legs, turtle eggs. They are delicious."

It did not take the Hopton children long to find the first nest, which the mother turtle had tried vainly to conceal. Her tracks were still clearly visible from and to the sea. In the nest were over two hundred eggs, about the size of bantam eggs and with flexible shells. Lewis ate several on the spot, but Margo did not find them appetizing.

Following along the dunes, Margo saw an unhappy sight. A huge sea turtle, surely several hundred pounds, lay dead on the beach. For amusement, someone had almost blown its head off with a load of buckshot. Margo could not imagine why anyone would shoot just for the thrill of killing.

Looking out to sea, Margo noticed that the ship she had seen on the horizon when they first reached the beach was now much closer and seemed headed toward them. She reached in her bag and took out her field glass, the only keepsake she still had from Gabriel. She had given his saber to Rowner and his compass to Leitner and had distributed his boots and uniforms among his men, but she kept his field glass as a keepsake and for bird watching. Focusing carefully, she noted that the ship was showing no colors.

"What kind of a ship is that?" she asked Lewis. "It doesn't have any flags. Could they be pirates?"

"Very possibly," he answered. "There are always a lot of pirates around when a war stops. All the privateers are suddenly out of the only job they know. Remember the corsair that brought in the Spanish merchant ship to Frederica and sold the cargo to Horton?"

"Yes I do. I bought a peacock feather fan at the sale."

"Well," Lewis continued, "when he got back to Newport he was acclaimed a hero and received an even larger ship to catch another prize. Sadly for him he was even more successful the second time."

"Why 'sadly'?" Margo asked.

"Because, when he returned to Newport he was hanged on a yard arm. The court wouldn't believe he didn't know that the peace had been signed. The war having ended, he was no longer a privateer but a common pirate. The British government is trying hard to convince the Spaniards that it's doing all it can to stop the English freebooters."

"Perhaps the captain of that ship hasn't heard the peace tidings either," Margo suggested. "Maybe it's Blackbeard."

"No chance of that," Lewis assured her. "Governor Rhett captured and hanged Teach several years before you were born."

"I see they've launched a longboat and are headed this way," Margo said apprehensively.

"Good, we can hide and see if they bury a treasure."

"I'm serious, Lewis. You may think it funny, but I'm scared. I don't like the looks of the men in that boat any more than I liked the Indians who visited us on our return from Augusta. It's getting late so we can end the picnic now and not frighten anyone about the pirates."

Realizing that Margo had every right to be afraid, and remembering her "condition", Lewis suggested an early departure because the tide was just right, and the wagons were quickly loaded. When their dugout reached Charleston, Lewis reported the suspicious vessel to the coast guard.

15

The Gilded Coach Arrives

Although Margo was merely the parson's wife and not qualified to hear confessions, many wives came to her for advice and comfort. The most common complaint was that their husbands visited houses of ill repute in Charleston or kept "high yaller" girls in the quarters. Margo recollected that, while visiting one of the neighboring plantations, she had seen family resemblances in the big house and the quarters. Still, remembering her unjust suspicions against Gabriel, she tried to convince the ladies that their worries were unfounded. Although they all feared the truth, she was still a great comfort.

Margo had been working on the Drum Plantation accounts for some weeks. The previous accountant had done an excellent job and had also coached his successor as long as necessary. Being a good Swiss with a strong aversion toward the kind of debts that ruined her poor father, Margo began to pay off as many debts as possible, even though that meant cutting down household allowances.

"Don't be so strict," Lewis pleaded. "Everyone on the delta lives on his deficits. It's a way of life here. If we didn't all borrow, we wouldn't have so many charming rich banker friends in Charleston to call on."

"Do you remember, when we were reading Hamlet, how much I liked the lines 'Neither a borrower nor a lender be, for loan oft loses both itself and friend, and borrowing dulls the edge of husbandry?' I think that is the way it ran. In any case, it's good advice, Lewis, my Love."

"You and Mrs. Horton must have read *Hamlet* often."

"Not very. But a line like that will stick in the mind of a Swiss. The French expression *faire le Suisse* means to 'play Scotch', that is, to be very, very frugal. And that 's the way this office is going to run things from now on."

Margo had made a solemn pact with Lewis, unbeknownst to him.

187

He was free to theologize and sermonize all he wished without interference from her, and in return he would not intrude into the plantation management. Lewis seemed pleased to be relieved of such mundane work. Actually, Margo did intrude on Lewis's sermonizing. Missing his company on Saturday afternoons, which he devoted to preparing his Sunday sermon, she speeded up the process by buying a copy of *Dr. Whitehead's Book of Christian Homilies*. She would pick out an appropriate sermon, summarize and alter it a bit, and then subtly work it into her conversation with her lord and master.

~

After a few months of keeping the plantation books, Margo was more or less running the plantation, at least with regard to its finances. Before making any decision about the actual operations she always consulted Elisha, and she let the hands know that he was still their boss. The first thing she did was to persuade Habersham to give her a large loan at seven and a half percent to pay off all the small outstanding debts.

"How did you get such a good rate?" the astonished husband asked. "Habersham usually gets ten percent."

"But such ten-percent loans are sometimes risky: his debtors frequently run away, leaving him their plantations, which are often less fertile than promised or are flooded too often to make a crop. He gave the lower rate because he knew that Drum Plantation is safe collateral."

Margo then paid off the many trifling ten-percent loans and began economizing to pay off the major debt as soon as possible. By the seventh month all was well with Margo's books and her pregnancy. The plantation's debt, now only a fraction of the plantation's real value, was rapidly declining, and she felt that she could relax a little.

"When you proposed to me," she reproached her husband, "you didn't say anything about any outside income. I expected to live abstemiously, as most parsons' wives must."

"I didn't want you to marry me for my money. I didn't want to be just a means for you to get your Gilded Coach. But you have done so well with your finances that you can have a gilded coach right now if you want it."

"Not a chance, but many thanks just the same. It would upset my bookkeeping and add a new debt. Besides that, I achieved my Gilded Coach way back on the day I first bathed in my copper bath tub. After that, there was really nothing else I wanted. I don't remember having had a Gilded Coach dream since then."

"I seem to have noticed that," Lewis agreed.

"When I rode in Edward's coach-and-four in Charleston, I felt so silly, like a fake jewel in a public showcase. You have already given me my Gilded Coach," Margo said, giving her husband an affectionate kiss. "Besides that, I first thought the Gilded Coach represented good food and fancy clothes. But I had all the food I could eat already at Fort Argyle, meat or fish every day. And the widow Horton gave me better clothes than any in our village. What the Gilded Coach really symbolized, although I didn't know it yet, was the ability to read, play the piano, and marry you."

❧

After admitting her condition on that stormy Voodoo night, Margo took good care of herself and, when not involved in book keeping, she lived the humdrum but enjoyable life of a country parson's wife, entertaining her parishioners at tea and visiting the sick. A few months after the hurricane the *Gazette* published the following note.

> The Rev. Lewis Middleton Delegal and his wife Margaret, the relict of Capt. Gabriel Bacques, announce the birth of their first child, who was baptized last Sunday as Lewis Middleton Delegal, Jr., Commissary Alexander Garden officiating.

There was no way for the *Gazette*'s editor to know that this child was to be the first of six. Some years later one of the Delegal slave women was heard boasting, "Miss Margo, she got six chillun, an dey all lib."